Mr. Crotchety

Rich Amooi

To receive updates on new releases, exclusive deals, and occasional silly stuff, sign up for Rich's newsletter at: http://www.richamooi.com/newsletter

To my wonderful, amazing, beautiful mother—who also happens to be a real estate agent. Thank you for making me possible.

Chapter One

"Smudge marks on the glass make me twitchy," said Roger Hudson, analyzing the display window in front of his shoe store. "Then I breakout in hives. You want to see my face looking like a pepperoni pizza?"

The teenage girl smiled. "No, Mr. Hudson."

"Of course not. Nobody does. And do you know what I'll do to you if I see a smudge mark on that window?"

She nodded. "You'll snap off my fingers and feed them to me one by one."

"Exactly. And how do you think your life would be without fingers?"

"A living hell."

"You've been paying attention. Good. And forget about the physical limitations—it's the mental anguish that'll eat you up like a turkey vulture feasting on fresh roadkill. Imagine not being able to text."

"I would die."

"You got *that* right. And people would call you Stubby behind your back. You want to be called Stubby?"

She bit her lower lip. "No, Mr. Hudson."

"Of course not. Nobody wants that. And get rid of that

smile—I'm being serious here."

The girl broke off a small piece of clear tape from the dispenser and placed it across the last corner of the poster, careful not to touch the glass. She stared through the shop window at her mom who stood on the sidewalk outside. The woman inspected the poster and gave her daughter an enthusiastic thumbs-up before returning to the conversation on her cell phone.

Roger squinted and pointed at the window. "Is that a smudge mark?"

"No, Mr. Hudson."

"Better not be. And quit being so polite. You're a prime target for people to walk all over you. If you disagree with someone, speak up. Always say what's on your mind."

"My mom said I had to be nice to you because you have issues."

Roger eyed her One Direction t-shirt and grunted. "Is that right?" He glared out to the street at the girl's mother who stopped talking on her phone again to mouth him a *thank you*.

"She thinks you're totally hot," said the girl. "But she said you lose your hotness whenever you open your mouth."

Roger blinked twice. "Forget what I said earlier about always saying what's on your mind." He flicked his hand in the direction of the door. "You can leave now."

The girl pointed to Roger's dog on his bed in the corner. "Can I say hi to Crouton?"

"He doesn't like humans."

She gave Roger an impressive boo-boo face. "Please?"

He sighed and pointed toward the cash register. "The bacon treats are behind the counter. Only one! He's starting to wobble when he walks."

The girl circled around the counter and grabbed the bag of treats. The pug heard the sound of the plastic bag and sprang to his feet, his curly little tail doing its best imitation of a wag. She pulled a bacon treat from the bag and held it about twelve inches above the dog's nose. "Sit, Crouton."

"Not gonna happen," said Roger. "He's just about the dumbest dog in the—"

Crouton sat and waited for his treat.

What the hell?

She gave Crouton the treat and ran her hand along his silky fawn coat. "You're a smart boy."

"Even a blind squirrel finds an acorn every now and then." Roger pointed to the door. "Don't keep your mom waiting."

The girl stood. "Thanks for letting us put the poster in the window."

Roger waved off her gratitude. "Don't do drugs and don't sleep around."

She rolled her eyes and left.

After the two walked away, Roger went outside to inspect the poster from the street. It promoted the annual walk to end cancer. He'd let them put a poster in his window the last five years.

Cancer.

He couldn't think of a single word in the English language he despised more.

"Are you open yet?" said the familiar voice behind Roger on the sidewalk.

Oh, God.

He swung around and there she was. Maggie "The Mouth" Madden.

The woman knew everything about everybody in Saratoga and Roger was certain it was her mission in life to bore him to death. To top it off, Maggie never bought shoes from him. Ever. He glanced down at her shoes and cringed.

Easy Spirit. Size nine. Circa 1985.

He gestured to the front door. "You know I'm open, Maggie. Come inside if you have to."

Maggie followed Roger inside and jumped right into her usual pretending-to-be-interested-in-something ritual. She walked around the large round display table in the center of the store and grabbed the Anne Klein metallic flat from the sales rack. She smelled the shoe and stuck it back in its place. As she wandered around his store she hummed a tune. Nice act. It would only be a matter of time before she told Roger about someone who was having an affair. Or a neighbor who bought a fancy new car that was worth more than her house. Or something else he didn't give a rat's ass about. Any second now.

"Guess what?" Maggie said.

Roger eyed her stomach. "You're pregnant?"

Maggie's eyes grew wide. "Do you know how old I am?"

He analyzed the sixty-five-year-old woman's pink dress and her matching fingernails. "Seventeen?"

Maggie blushed and placed her hand on her chest. "Roger Hudson, are you flirting with me?"

Kill me now.

"Speaking of love . . ." She smiled and continued. "Did you hear Chastity Monds is getting married again?"

"No."

"There's still hope for you."

Right.

A great love came around once in a lifetime and Roger had already had it. Thirty years of glorious marriage to Macy, his college sweetheart from Santa Clara University. He wasn't in the market for another woman. Not now. Not ever.

"Did you hear Dr. Jenkins was caught roller-skating half-naked in the middle of the night on Prospect Road?"

Don't act shocked. It'll just motivate her to stay and gossip longer. It's no big deal whatsoever that your doctor is a freak.

Roger shrugged. "Nothing wrong with a little exercise."

Maggie did a double take. "Without clothes?"

"Smart man—less to wash. I hate doing laundry."

Maggie blew out a desperate breath. "He was wearing his nurse's bra!"

Note to self: find a new doctor.

"You can never have too much support," said Roger. "The guy's got some serious man-boobs."

Maggie shook her head in disgust. "Sometimes I think you're not even listening to me." She spotted someone out the window and perked up. "I'll be right back."

"I'm not going anywhere."

Unfortunately.

Roger wanted a peaceful day, that's all. He'd be happy with just a couple of sales before heading across the street for his usual tuna sandwich. His cell phone rang on the counter and he walked over, glancing down at the caller ID.

His sister Brenda again.

She had called this morning at the butt crack of dawn and left a message. Something about Roger's nephew Jeffrey wanting to visit again for the summer. He loved his nephew to death, but he was in no mood for company. Not from anybody.

"Hi, Brenda."

"You don't love your nephew anymore?" she asked.

"What a question."

"Well then? Why didn't you call me back?"

"I . . . think . . . we . . . have . . . a . . . bad . . . connection."

"Don't give me that crap, Roger. How about if I tell Jeffrey that you have no interest in seeing him this year? Yeah —I like that plan. Talk to you later."

"Hang on!"

Roger's sister was a master at making him feel guilty. He didn't need her for that. He was perfectly capable of feeling guilty on his own. He dropped the phone down to his side and paced back and forth through the store. He took a deep breath and let it out slowly. He adjusted the leather Steve Madden ankle boot on the wall display that wasn't straight. Then he adjusted it again. And again.

"Roger?"

"This isn't a good time."

"It *never* is."

He didn't answer. He couldn't argue with that.

"Do you love your nephew enough to let him stay with you for a little bit? Yes or no. It's a simple question."

Roger sighed. "Fine. I love him more than life itself. Happy?"

"Very! I knew you'd come to your senses. This will be good for you."

"You don't have to keep trying to convince me—I said yes. When will he be here?"

"Any minute."

Roger jerked his head back. "What?"

The front door to the shop swung open and in walked his nephew. "Uncle Roger!"

Unbelievable.

Roger's sister had set him up.

Crouton popped up from his bed and sprinted in Jeffrey's direction. "Arf! Arf!"

Jeffrey reached down and scooped up the dog and was greeted with the customary licks. "Good to see you too, Crouton. It's been way too long."

"Remind me to kill you later," whispered Roger into the phone before he hung up on his sister.

Roger eyed his nephew. It wasn't a surprise that people thought Jeffrey was his son. They had so many similar characteristics. Both were exactly six feet tall. Both around the same build, wide shoulders and slim waists. Brown eyes. Black hair, although Roger had a decent amount of the gray mixed in now. Heck, they even shared the same shoe size—eleven.

Jeffrey had a smile on his face wider than the suitcase he lugged. He set Crouton on the floor and approached his uncle with arms wide open.

He gave Roger a heart-felt embrace. "Good to see you."

"You, too."

This was the truth. As much as Roger tried to avoid being social, his nephew was his favorite person on earth. It was always a pleasure to see him. Jeffrey was a kind, smart, and loving kid. Hell, he wasn't even a kid anymore.

Where have the years gone?

Roger felt a little emotional.

He pulled away and slapped Jeffrey on the arm. "You came to free-load off your uncle again?"

Jeffrey smiled. "Nobody makes hamburgers like you. Or spinach omelets. Or fresh guacamole."

"Sounds like I'll be cooking full-time. How long are you staying?"

"Long enough for me to earn some extra money and also make a dent in my thesis."

"Right. That."

Jeffrey was writing a thesis on human behavior at San Diego State. He was home for the summer and wanted to study Roger's interaction with customers as part of the research for his behavioral neuroscience master's degree.

"You can study all you want," said Roger. "But when you're in my shop you're working. Got it?"

"Not a problem. Actually, I'm going to have two jobs while I'm here. Selling shoes. And outselling you."

"Not gonna happen."

Jeffrey laughed. "Your social skills have deteriorated over the last few years, so this should be easy, Uncle Caveman."

Roger rolled Jeffrey's suitcase out of the way behind the counter. "I guess I should get used to you sticking me under a microscope since you're studying that psychology gibberish. Let's just get this out of the way right here and now. You're going to tell me I need to get a life, right? That I need to quit being so antisocial?"

Jeffrey shook his head. "Not at all."

Roger studied his nephew for a moment. "Oh . . ."

This wouldn't be so bad after all if Jeffrey wasn't going to give Roger advice every ten minutes. Still, Jeffrey had a grin on his face. He was holding back something.

"Say it," said Roger.

"Nothing. I don't think you're antisocial at all."

Good.

His nephew had gotten wiser over the last year. Roger's shoulders relaxed.

"You're unsociable," Jeffrey added. "There's a big difference."

Roger's shoulders tensed up again. "No need to explain. You hungry? How about you go grab an early lunch?"

Jeffrey ignored him. "If you're antisocial you're opposed to the founding principles of society. *You*, on the other hand, are reluctant to engage with others due to something in the past that has traumatized you. That's completely different. You're unsociable."

"Should I kill you now or let you have one more meal?"

"Yes!" screamed Sally Bright.

She popped up from her chair and circled the giant mahogany table in the conference room, dishing out high-fives to the other real estate agents along the way. Back at her chair she gripped the edge of the table with both hands. "I feel a little light-headed."

Sally bounced with excitement. She'd just learned in the office meeting that her dream house—the one she had loved ever since she was a little girl—would be on the market soon.

She had fond memories of that home. One of her favorite things to do was swing from the giant tree in their front yard. William and Tammy Fusco—the present owners of the home—never had kids but they had always spoiled the children they came in contact with. They were good people who always put a smile on her face, and more importantly, in her heart.

The agents laughed as Sally's best friend and co-worker, Portia Channing, jokingly fanned her with a manila folder. "Breathe! You're going to be okay!"

Sally's boss Phillip stood up and clapped his hands. "Okay, meeting's over. Everyone have a productive day. And someone get Sally some oxygen."

The agents laughed again and filed out of the conference room, leaving Sally and Portia alone.

Sally hugged Portia. "This is amazing." She'd waited forever to buy this house and she would finally have the opportunity. It felt like a dream. "Tell me everything. When? Why? How?"

"Do you want me to find you a paper bag to breathe into?" asked Portia.

Sally couldn't contain herself. "Tell me!"

Portia laughed. "Fine! The Fuscos are moving down to Palm Springs. Some gated community with golf, swimming, and Monday night bingo. Anyway, the house should go on the market in a few weeks."

"Is it your listing?"

Portia shook her head. "They have a relative who's an agent." She flashed Sally a smile. "Are you really going to buy it?"

"What's my favorite word?"

"Yes?"

"Yes! Of course I'm going to buy it."

It had been her plan ever since she had told her father she wanted to live in that house. Of course, her father's response was not what she had expected and she had cried that day.

That's not realistic, Sally. People like us can't afford a house like that.

She loved her dad with all her heart and he was a good man, but something about what he'd said bugged her. Why couldn't she have that house? Why couldn't she work hard and achieve whatever dreams she wanted to achieve?

As if Portia had read her mind she rubbed Sally's shoulder. "Too bad your dad isn't around to see you do it."

"Yeah. But the goal was never to prove him wrong. I guess it's always been more to prove that I could do it. Plus, I've always been in love with that house!"

The Fuscos threw the most wonderful parties in their backyard. They used to hang Japanese paper lanterns from the trees in the summer. Beautiful colors that lit up at night . . . green, red, blue, pink, orange, white. Sally would stare up into them and pretend the lanterns were planets and she was traveling through space.

Sally's adrenaline was pumping now. She hadn't waited this long for nothing. It was time to come up with a plan to make it happen and make sure it was doable. Real estate prices in Silicon Valley had sky-rocketed, but she knew she could afford the monthly mortgage. Qualifying for the loan —that was a different story. She would need a sizable down payment to make it a sure thing.

"Do you know the price?" asked Sally.

"No. Let's check the MLS."

"Yes! Great idea."

They sat down at the conference table; Sally swung her laptop around and opened it. She logged into the Multiple Listing Service website and punched in the address for the Fuscos' home.

Sally's smile grew wider as she read the status. "Coming soon."

"Oh." Portia pointed to the price on the monitor. "That's on the high side, isn't it?"

"A little bit."

It wasn't cheap, but Sally would find a way to make it happen. She'd busted her butt and sold more houses than anyone in her office. She had saved just about every penny and had a sizable savings account. Then her father got sick. Since he didn't have insurance she ended up using over half of her savings to pay for his medical bills and funeral. Still, she was confident she could make it happen. She pulled out her calculator and did some calculations.

"Hmm," she said.

"What?" asked Portia.

"I'm going to be a little short on the down payment."

"How short? Maybe I can cover the difference."

Sally squeezed Portia's hand. "You're so sweet."

She wasn't surprised Portia made that offer. They'd been best friends for over twenty years and had been through everything together. Sally's marriage. Sally's divorce. Portia's marriage. Portia's divorce. And of course the darkest moment when Sally found out she had breast cancer. She would've never made it through that period without Portia's love and support. It was a thousand times harder than the divorce. In fact, the divorce was a carnival compared to the cancer.

Sally did a few more calculations and then held the calculator in front of Portia's face.

Portia lost her smile. "Okay, maybe I won't be able to help you. I'm sorry."

"No worries! I think I just need two transactions to make this happen. Ideally, I need to find a client who wants me to sell their home *plus* find them a new one. The commissions from both will give me more than enough money to add to the down payment."

"Any leads?"

"Not yet!"

"Well, with your luck something will magically drop out of the sky."

Chapter Two

Roger watched the employee at Highway 9 Sandwiches prepare his lunch order. It was his favorite place, located directly across the street from his shoe store. The kid copped an attitude after he messed up Roger's sandwich the first time and was remaking it.

How difficult can it be?

Whole grain bread. Tuna. Tomato. Cheddar cheese. Onions. Avocado. Barbecue sauce.

Roger ordered the same sandwich every day. It wasn't rocket science. He knew it wouldn't be long before the kid got distracted again by a girl walking by. Or that irritating boom-boom-boom racket that came out of the stereo system. If he could reach those speakers he would have yanked them out of the wall by now.

The employee grabbed the mayonnaise and—

Roger cleared his throat. "Barbecue sauce."

The kid avoided eye contact and sighed. "I *know* that. I was moving the bottle over *here*." He placed the mayonnaise on the other side of the sandwich board where it clearly wasn't supposed to go. Then he grabbed the barbecue sauce and squirted it across the top of the tuna.

"Why don't you just admit it when you make a mistake?" said Roger. "Like your parents did after you were born."

The kid glared at him and slapped two slices of cheddar on the bread. "And why don't you admit you're a crotchety old geezer?"

"I admit it. Your turn."

The kid laughed. "I didn't make a mistake."

The truth was Roger had been called just about everything in the book. Geezer. Jerk. Bastard. Dick. Prick. Schmuck. Grumpy. Cranky. And of course, crotchety. And they were all right. He was all of those. But he had every right to be, after what he'd been through.

He paid the pain-in-the-ass kid and grabbed the tray with his sandwich, chips, and root beer. He sat at his usual table outside on the sidewalk. He glanced across the street and could see Jeffrey helping a customer. He wouldn't be surprised if his nephew sold a pair of shoes today. He was a very likable kid and as smart as anyone. He'd helped Roger last summer and learned a lot about the shoe business.

Roger enjoyed a few bites of his sandwich and washed it down with a gulp of root beer.

Peace. That's all I want.

"What a beautiful day!" screamed a woman with what must have been a bull horn aimed directly at his ear.

He jumped up in his seat and his hand smacked the edge of the sandwich basket, catapulting his tuna sandwich into the air. Roger reached out and fumbled with the sandwich, miraculously able to grab a hold of it before it hit the cement.

The woman clapped her hands. "Nice catch!"

Roger gave the stink eye to Miss Ham and Swiss—also known as Sally Bright. Sally was a real estate agent from down the street at Big Basin Homes. She was elegant, classy, and self-confident.

She was also the most annoyingly positive person Roger knew.

Well, he didn't personally *know* her but he did know just about everything about her since she never grasped the concept of volume control during conversations at lunch. And any info he didn't get direct from Sally's trap was graciously delivered by Maggie the Mouth.

This much he had learned from Maggie. Sally was divorced. Fifty years old. Successful. The rest he could see for himself. Attractive. Petite. Short brown hair with brown eyes. But he had no interest in the opposite sex. And fortunately, he'd learned to mentally put on the blinders and picture her as a rotten tomato. It worked most of the time except when he caught a glimpse of those dynamite legs of hers. That was only because he wanted to check out her shoes and he always started at the legs, naturally.

But something didn't seem right with Sally—like she was hiding something. She gave off the illusion that she never had a bad day, but he didn't buy her act.

No way in hell anyone can be that happy all the time.

She wasted food, too. He couldn't figure out if it was because she was always in such a damn hurry or because she was on a strict diet, but she never finished the second half of her sandwich. Like clockwork, every day, she left it on the table. One of these days he'd call her on it. But that would involve talking with her and *that* he didn't want to do.

Sally slid by Roger in her well-pressed navy blue dress suit and he glanced down at her legs. He continued farther down to her shoes.

Naturalizer. Size six. Good quality. Affordable.

As she disappeared inside he wondered why she didn't buy shoes at his store. Roger had the best brands for women and offered competitive prices. He believed people should support their local businesses and she didn't. Well, except for the sandwich place.

A few minutes later Sally came out with her ham and Swiss on focaccia, light on the mayo, and iced tea. She ordered the same thing every day. Just like he did.

She sat at the empty table next to Roger. "This looks like a great spot."

Don't talk with her.

Sally smiled at Roger—like she always did. And Roger pretended he didn't notice her—like he always did. He wasn't going to fall into her trap. Every single day the woman tried to engage in a conversation with him. Why couldn't she get the hint that he didn't want to talk to her? Or anybody else for that matter? He knew if he acknowledged anything she did, the flood gates would open up and thousands of adjectives and exclamation points would flow in his direction, pulling him under to his death.

Roger had seen Sally's name in the paper after she'd won top agent in Silicon Valley a few years ago. Pretty impressive considering how many agents there were. She was one of the regulars he saw almost every day at Highway 9 Sandwiches. At least Sally had good taste in food. Nobody made fresh bread like Highway 9 Sandwiches.

A gust of wind kicked up and blew Sally's napkin off her lap. It flew toward Roger and stuck to one of his kneecaps. He peeled the napkin from his knee and handed it back to her, careful to not make any eye contact.

"Thank you," said Sally. "You're so sweet."

"Like a lemon," mumbled Roger.

"I *love* lemons!"

We need a distraction. An earthquake would be fantastic right about now.

"Do you have a lemon tree, Roger?"

Yeah, she knew his name. No big deal. It was a small city and he owned one of the businesses there.

One of the businesses she didn't shop at.

Roger knew the names of the business owners in the area, so it made sense she knew his name. Either that or she got his name from Maggie. Whatever the reason, this was the first time she'd ever called him by name. But he wasn't going to engage in a conversation with her.

Sally leaned closer to Roger. "It looks like you're not in the mood to talk."

"Brains and beauty. A rare combination."

Crap. That almost sounded like a compliment. Don't do that.

"Thank you!" said Sally. "You're so sweet."

"Don't call me that."

Roger kept his head down and continued to eat. Almost done. He ate at Highway 9 Sandwiches every single day because of their bread, but he needed to find a better place. Right. Wasn't going to happen. It would be easier to lower his standards.

"Roger," said Sally.

Roger finished the last bite and just needed to polish off the last few chips. Then he was out of there.

"*Roger*," Sally repeated.

The woman sounded like a parrot.

"*Roger*," Sally repeated one more time.

He stuck the empty chip bag in the basket and turned his head. "What?"

"You know . . ." Sally smiled. "If you ever need to talk about anything. Anything at all . . ."

"Geez Louise, I already get plenty of psychology crap from my family members."

Sally shrugged. "Okay, well, the offer is always open."

"And what makes you think you're qualified to give me advice?"

Sally studied Roger for a few moments. "I never said I

was going to give you advice."

She's right. She never said that. *Idiot.*

"What's the deal with you, anyway?" asked Roger. "Do you celebrate your birthday every day or something?"

"Of course not. Although that wouldn't be such a bad idea!"

"Did you win the lottery?"

"I don't play the lottery. Why are you asking me these silly questions?"

"I'm just trying to figure out why you're so damn happy all the time."

Sally smiled. "I love life. I'm happy to be alive. Isn't that reason enough?"

"Sell your sugar somewhere else—I'm not buying it."

"Nobody is asking you to buy it."

"You act like you can poop rainbows if you wanted. Well, I can see through you. It's all a show."

"We both know who's putting on a show and it certainly isn't me. And I'm totally okay if you want to believe I'm not a happy person because I live my life for me, not for anybody else." She got up and grabbed her purse. "I hope you have an amazing day."

"Of course you do. I wish they served pancakes here because they'd go perfect with all that syrup you're spewing."

She winked at Roger. "I *love* pancakes."

"Not a surprise. You love everything!"

Sally didn't acknowledge his last comment and

disappeared up the street.

Roger stood, fuming. Why had he talked to her? He knew better. He grabbed the other half of Sally's sandwich before the employee came around to clean her table. He wrapped it tighter to keep the sandwich fresh.

"You shouldn't waste food," he mumbled.

Roger headed down the sidewalk a few doors to the gas station on the corner. He walked by the bathrooms behind the building and around past the garbage dumpster to the row of large bushes near the brick wall. He turned sideways and scooted between two of the bushes until he got to the clearance on the other side. He glanced down at the homeless man sleeping on the ground and placed the sandwich on top of his backpack. Roger snuck back through the bushes and brushed some dust off his shirt before returning to the shoe shop.

Upon his entering the shop Crouton sprinted in his direction, the little guy jumping up toward his thighs like Crouton was on a trampoline. "Arf! Arf!"

"Settle down." Roger picked up the dog up and petted him on the head. "You act like I traveled around the world and left you here to rot." Crouton aimed for Roger's face to give him a wet kiss, but Roger held him tight so he couldn't reach. "I don't need your slobber on my face." He set Crouton down and glanced at his nephew.

Jeffrey shot Roger a grin like he'd been up to something.

"What?" said Roger.

"Nothing. Except I had three sales while you were gone."

"In forty minutes?"

Jeffrey grinned and nodded.

"Impossible. I was watching from across the street and only saw one person enter and leave."

Jeffrey pointed toward the drawer. "Check the receipts then if you don't believe your honest and handsome nephew."

"I'll give you the handsome part but that's about it."

Roger walked behind the counter and pulled open the drawer underneath the cash register. He grabbed the receipts envelope and peeked inside. He glanced at Jeffrey who was still grinning, then turned his attention back to the envelope, pulling the receipts out.

"Huh," said Roger, nodding. "Three receipts."

"Maybe four," said Jeffrey, pointing his head toward the street.

Not again.

The Mouth had returned.

"Please don't come in," said Roger. "Don't touch the door handle."

"Wishing for people not to enter your store?" said Jeffrey. "That's not a good business model. The second reason why sales have been slow."

"Right. What was the first reason?"

"You being unsociable."

"Oh. That." Roger blew out a deep breath. "She's not

even a potential customer—Maggie never buys a thing. Ever."

"Mind if I give it a shot?"

Roger laughed. "Go for it."

Jeffrey waved Maggie inside and her eyes lit up when she spotted him through the window.

"Look at you!" said Maggie, approaching Jeffrey and hugging him. She checked him out from head to toe and smiled. "You get more handsome every year. Just like your Uncle Roger."

"Thank you. So glad you came in—let's get you some new shoes."

"Oh." Maggie looked around the store. "Not today."

Roger fought back the urge to laugh.

Jeffrey scratched his chin and eyed her shoes. "Sorry. I just assumed you wanted to replace those shoes since the right one is more worn than the left. You're smart enough to know that can cause back problems. My bad. I guess I shouldn't assume health is at the top of everyone's—"

"Back problems?" She looked down at her shoes. "Oh, dear. That's the last thing I want. My good friend Gladys has had nothing but back problems this year and doesn't even leave the house anymore! Can you imagine that? I don't know what I'd do if I was cooped up all day long." Maggie glanced around the store again. "What do you suggest?" She gestured to her feet. "They just don't make shoes like these anymore."

Jeffrey smiled. "I've got just the thing. You'll feel like you're walking on marshmallows. And your back will thank you!"

Maggie pinched Jeffrey's cheek. "You're such a good boy. I think your old uncle can learn a thing or two from you."

I taught him everything he knows! Well, almost everything.

Fifteen minutes later Jeffrey had his fourth sale of the day. Maggie had bought the pair of Dr. Scholl's that Jeffrey had recommended plus a second pair in a different color. If his nephew's smile was any wider his face would have snapped in half from the pressure. Roger opened the drawer to stick the receipt in the envelope.

"Thanks again, Maggie," said Jeffrey. "I'd recommend going through your shoes in the closet and throwing out any of them that are worn like these." He dropped her old shoes in the trash canister next to the register. They made a loud clanking sound. "When did you buy these, anyway?"

"Hmm. I can't be too sure. I think it was right around when *Miami Vice* was on television. Or was it *Dukes of Hazard?* I'm better at remembering current events."

Ain't that the truth.

"No worries." Jeffrey handed her the shopping bag and walked her to the door. "Just glad you're headed in the right direction. Nothing is more important than your health."

"You've opened my eyes!" she said. "You're right. Health first. I'll be back to get more shoes from you tomorrow. But just a couple more pairs to start." She pinched Jeffrey's cheek. "I do okay, but I'm not loaded with money like that billionaire who bought the house next door to your uncle."

Jeffrey opened the door for Maggie and—

"Wait a minute!" said Roger, rushing toward Maggie. "What are you talking about?"

Maggie stepped back inside the store. "Pardon me?"

"What billionaire?"

"You didn't know? I thought you'd be the first to know!"

"It's obvious I don't know, so tell me."

"Mark Brannah bought the house next door to you."

"Who is Mark Brannah?"

Maggie set her bag on the floor. "You know, Mark Brannah? That high tech CEO known for throwing lavish parties until the wee hours of the morning?"

"Why the hell would he buy that house? It's barely two thousand square feet."

"Fortunately I have that info for you. He bought it for the land since it has a two acre lot. He plans to level the house and build a mega mansion there, twenty thousand square feet or something outrageous like that. It's going to be the largest house in Saratoga."

Please. No.

Roger paced back and forth. "This can't be happening. All I want is peace and quiet. And that bastard is going to take away the morning sun in my backyard!"

"Don't forget the weekly parties with live music!" she said with way too much enthusiasm. "Don't worry, I'm sure you'll be on the invite list."

Roger's peaceful home life was about the only thing he looked forward to. He loved his morning coffee on the back patio. And barbecuing in the evening. Sure, they were usually barbecues for one person, but who cared? And he loved to leave the bedroom window open at night. How would he be able to sleep with so much noise coming from next door? This was the worst possible news ever and there was only one thing he could do.

"I'm moving," said Roger. "I'm selling my house."

"Wow," said Jeffrey. "That was a fast decision, but why the rush? It'll take at least a year before they finish building it."

Roger shook his head. "That's a year or more of construction noise and dust. No way. I can't handle that. I'm going to get a real estate agent immediately and sell the house."

Maggie's eyes grew wide. "Call Sally Bright! She'll help you sell the house and she's the sweetest thing ever! Single, too."

Roger blinked. "I'd rather be kicked in the balls repeatedly until I pass out."

Chapter Three

The next day Roger waited in the conference room at Big Basin Homes. He'd received confirmation from two different people that what Maggie had told him was correct. That idiot had purchased the property next door and was going to tear it down and build a mansion. No way in hell Roger was going to live there now. He would sell his house immediately and find something new.

Jeffrey was back at the store taking care of business while Roger's only goal was to get a real estate agent contracted to put the house on the market. He realized now that Jeffrey visiting was the best thing that could have happened. Without him the store would be closed at this very moment. That's how motivated Roger was to sell his house. Yes, he'd had many wonderful memories in his place but he tried to block that from his brain, so he wouldn't change his mind about moving.

Roger had already interviewed two agents and they were both a bust. The first agent smelled funny so that was a hell-no from the get-go. Agent number two kept sneezing during the meeting and one of those times Roger even felt spray hit his hands. Eliminated.

He waited for the third agent, who was late. This was turning out to be a crappy day.

He checked his watch again. It was fifteen minutes past the agreed appointment time with Portia Channing. He tapped his pen on the table as he went through her info. One of the top agents in the office three out of the last five years. Top lister last year. Member of the Platinum Club, whatever that was. These things meant zilch to him if she couldn't keep her appointment time. Arrive when you say you're going to arrive. What's so difficult about that?

He tapped the pen on the table a few more times before he spotted Miss Ham and Swiss. She approached another agent on the other side of the glass for a chat. Thank God she was distracted and didn't notice Roger. His eyes traveled down her shapely legs to her shoes.

Nine West. Size six. Comfortable. Reasonable price.

Roger knew she was good at her job but there was no way in hell he was ever going to hire her. Sally obviously drank gallons of caffeinated beverages all day long. Or she was high on something. Whatever the reason, he knew it would only be a matter of time before he killed her. And making the newspaper for murder wouldn't be good for his shoe business.

Roger clicked his pen a few times and the conference room door swung open.

"So sorry to keep you waiting," said Portia. She was out of breath.

While she opened her briefcase on the table Roger shot a quick glance at her shoes.

Christian Louboutin. Top of the line. Size eight.

They shook hands and both sat.

Portia pulled some papers from her briefcase. "I'm sorry. My lunch ran over and I got here as fast as I could."

"You were late because you were eating?"

Portia studied Roger for a moment. "Uh . . . yeah. A business lunch."

Roger stood up. "I'm sorry, this isn't going to work out."

"What?" Portia jumped up. "Wait, please sit down. I'm truly sorry."

"I need an agent who values my business."

"I *do* value your business."

"More than food?"

Portia burst out in laughter. "What?"

Roger just stared at her.

Portia stopped laughing and cleared her throat. "Wow, you're serious."

"Of course I'm serious. My time is valuable and I need someone who can respect that. I only wanted fifteen minutes of your time and you had all day to eat. Good day."

Roger grabbed his notes and pen from the table. He walked out of the conference room and ran straight into Sally. "Watch where you're going, Miss Happy."

"I was standing still," she said.

He blew out a deep breath. "Then watch where you're

standing."

Roger maneuvered around Sally and headed toward the front door.

<<<>>>

Sally turned and watched Roger Hudson leave. She checked out his tight butt and sighed.

What a complete waste of a good-looking man.

She stared through the glass of the conference room window. Portia waved her in.

Sally pushed open the glass door and stepped inside. "What happened?"

"Something giant got lodged up that man's ass, that's what happened. He's unbelievable. Yeah, he lost his wife from cancer, but does that give him the right to treat everyone like shit?"

Sally shrugged. "That has to be the most horrible feeling in the world, losing a loved one. Poor guy."

"Yeah, well, that poor guy wants to sell his house and buy a new one."

"How come you didn't meet him in his home?"

"He didn't want to. And nobody, including me, had the guts to tell him that interviewing multiple agents from the same office, in their office, is not how it's typically done."

"How many people did he interview?"

"He talked to Phillip and lined up three agents. And in

case you're wondering, he was very specific and told Phillip no brunettes. Otherwise you would've been selected to be interviewed."

"No brunettes? That's odd."

"Not really. His wife was a brunette."

Too bad. Roger would've been the ideal client for Sally. With the market the way it was she could easily sell his house and find him a new one in the same week. That commission would give her more than enough for the down payment on the Fuscos' property.

"What happened in your interview?"

Portia sighed. "Not much. I was the third out of the three agents interviewed. But I was late and he didn't like it. I'm pretty busy anyway, so that's okay. Let's forget about that. What's happening with you? Any leads?"

"No. And I crunched the numbers again and I definitely need two transactions to be able to buy the house. I may have to hit the streets and knock on some doors again. It's too late to do a mailing campaign. But something will come up—I'm sure of it."

Her dad's words came back into her head.

People like us can't afford a house like that.

Those words motivated her now more than ever.

"Why not work for Mr. Crotchety?"

Sally laughed. "I think he'd kill you if he found out you were calling him that. And no, he didn't want me since I wasn't one of the agents he interviewed. Anyway, I'm pretty sure he has something against me. I see the guy almost every day at lunch and I've tried talking to him. But he just grunts and continues eating."

Portia laughed. "Seriously, if anyone can handle that man it's you. Of course I mean *handle* in a non-sexual way. I know the guy's attractive but he's got the personality of a rattlesnake."

"Be nice."

"See how sweet you are? The guy is a total jerk and you're defending him."

"He's been through a lot. He'll learn, sooner or later."

Portia crossed her arms and frowned. "How much do you want that dream house of yours?"

"You know how much."

"Then you need to get that man as a client. Do whatever it takes. Hell, dye your hair! I think you would look fab as a blonde."

"Not gonna happen."

"Fine. Don't dye your hair. But you don't have a lot of time on your side. Walking door to door will take forever and is like trying to find a client in a haystack. Just go down to his shop and pretend you need some shoes. Then try to slip real estate into the conversation. But don't try to sell him your services because he won't go for it. You need to let it be his idea that you're going to be his agent."

"Are you serious?"

"Trust me. He's a man and that means he's got an ego

the size of California."

"Not all men have egos like that." Sally had a serious look on her face and then burst into laughter. "I tried to hold it as long as I could."

Portia and Sally shared a good laugh together.

"You're the best," said Sally, hugging Portia. "Thank you."

"You can thank me when you get your new house and cook me up some of my favorite pasta in your new kitchen."

"Deal!"

Portia was right. Why not go for it and try to get Roger Hudson's business? It was a great idea and tomorrow she would pay him a visit after lunch. She was certain she could handle the guy no matter how crotchety he was.

Chapter Four

The next day Sally sat across from Roger at Highway 9 Sandwiches. She tried engaging him in conversation more than a few times, but he was in grunt-mode again.

"Did you hear it was going to get up to a hundred degrees today?" she asked.

Grunt.

"The bread tastes extra fresh."

Grunt.

"Is that a new watch?"

Grunt.

"You sure are grunting a lot."

Grunt.

Sally had eaten slower than normal so Roger would leave before her. Then she'd wait a few minutes, cross the street, and enter his store for Operation: I Want To Sell Your House. She finished her lunch and felt awkard sitting there with nothing to do.

Eat your sandwich faster, Roger!

She went inside Highway 9 to pretend to use the restroom. Hopefully he'd be gone when she returned. A few minutes later Sally came out of the restroom and stopped.

You've got to be kidding me?

Roger had taken the rest of her sandwich from the table. She slid to the side behind one of the columns and peeked to see what he was up to. He looked around and then refolded the sandwich wrapper. Was he going to eat that later? Was he still hungry? Maybe he had money problems and couldn't afford another sandwich.

She exited the building after Roger disappeared out of view.

Where did he go?

She looked down the street to the right just as Roger cut through the gas station parking lot. About a minute or so later he came back out from behind the gas station and crossed the street. Odd. He didn't have the sandwich anymore. She ducked back inside Highway 9 until he entered his store and then she took off toward the gas station. She had no idea why she was so curious, but she had to know what he did with the other half of her sandwich. Had he given it to the gas station employee? A stray dog? Had he gone over there and eaten it out of view?

She cut through the lot behind the trash dumpster and stopped. It didn't make sense. She turned around and stared at the bushes in front of the brick wall. There was an opening in the middle of the bushes. She made sure there wasn't anyone watching and snuck through to the other side.

Sally certainly wasn't expecting what she saw. A homeless man slept on the ground on top of a comforter. To his side was the rest of her sandwich on top of a backpack.

"Unbelievable," she said.

The homeless man mumbled something and she quickly slid through the bushes back into the gas station parking lot. She crossed the street and walked toward Roger's shoe store.

Sally smiled. "Mr. Crotchety is not who he seems."

Roger was going to have a heart attack. Miss Ham and Swiss, Sally Bright, the most annoying woman in the world, stood directly outside of his store. Was she going to enter? That would be a first.

"Don't come in," said Roger. "Stay away."

Jeffrey added a new shoe to the sales rack. "Uncle Roger."

Roger was focused on Sally. "Keep moving. We're all out of shoes." Maybe he could send her a subliminal message. "Nothing to see here. Go away. Shoo. Skedaddle. Scram."

"You realize I'm going to have to use this information in my thesis?" He grabbed his notebook and scribbled a few things. "Good stuff."

The door swung open and Sally stepped inside. "I've been meaning to come in here forever! I can't believe this is the first time."

"We're closed!" blurted out Roger, a little too loudly.

He startled the hell out of Crouton and the dog jumped

up. "Arf! Arf!"

"Closed?" Sally reached down and petted Crouton.

Jeffrey laughed nervously. "What he meant to say is we're *close* to a record sales day. Everyone seems to be in the mood to buy shoes today."

She studied Jeffrey. "Me, too! I'm Sally Bright. I'm an agent for Big Basin homes, just up the street."

Jeffrey offered his hand. "I'm Jeffrey. This is my Uncle Roger's store, but he's kind enough to let me work here in the summer during my college break. Honestly, he doesn't need the help at all—he's been running this place for years all by himself."

"That's very sweet of him," she said, sounding surprised.

She locked eyes with Roger then dropped her gaze to Crouton. "What a cute little dog."

"His name is Crouton."

Sally laughed and scratched him under the chin. "You have such a funny little face, don't you? And a funny name too!" Crouton rolled over on his back and exposed his tummy. She petted the dog on his chest and then stood back up. "Adorable. Is he yours?"

"Nope." Jeffrey pointed to Roger.

Sally squished her eyebrows together. "I didn't picture Roger as a dog person."

"You'd be surprised," said Jeffrey. "He spoils Crouton. In fact, you should see what he has at home for—"

"All right, all right," said Roger. "This is a business so

Jeffrey please help the customer."

Roger pretended to search for something behind the cash register but snuck a peek at Sally's legs.

"Right," said Jeffrey, giving Roger the you-need-to-calm-down-before-you-scare-her-away look. "Can I help you find something today, Miss Bright?"

Sally glanced around the store and then turned back to Jeffrey. "Please call me Sally." She paused and Roger looked up, holding her gaze. "I was hoping your Uncle Roger could help me."

Roger swallowed hard. He couldn't find words to express how much he didn't want that to happen.

"Absolutely!" said Jeffrey. "All yours, uncle."

Damn.

Roger stepped forward and forced a smile. "Uh . . . anything in particular today?"

"These are nice," she said, pointing to the black pumps on the main display table. "I need something for work."

He shook his head. "Not the best choice."

"Pardon me?" said Sally.

Jeffrey cleared his throat and Roger looked over. His nephew was taking notes.

Great.

"I don't recommend them," continued Roger. "Don't get me wrong, they're great shoes." He grabbed a shoe from the display behind him and handed it to her. "This particular shoe is *much* better."

She raised an eyebrow. "It looks exactly like the other one."

"Not quite. These have the most advanced support technology available. You'll notice the comfort even after many hours on your feet."

She nodded. "And because of this amazing support it's twice the price of the first one, right?"

Roger shook his head. "Thirty percent less."

"Oh." She studied Roger, as if this were some sort of trap. He'd seen that look before. He was just being honest and making sure his clients got the best shoes for their money.

He took the shoe back from her. "You said you needed them for work, so I assumed you planned on doing a lot of walking in these. That's why I recommended them."

"Absolutely. I'm always running around during my day, picking up clients, showing them homes for sale. I even walk door to door occasionally to get face time with potential clients. I work hard and the days can be long, so I need comfortable shoes."

"Trust me." Roger held up the shoe for Jeffrey to see. "Can you grab me a size six?"

"You got it," said Jeffrey. He disappeared into the stockroom behind the register.

"How did you know my size?"

"It's my job." Roger gestured to the chair next to the full-length mirror. "Please have a seat."

"Thank you," said Sally. She sat, kicked off her shoes and waited.

Roger tried his hardest not to look at her feet but he couldn't help it. They were the cutest little things.

Sally cleared her throat.

She must think I'm a freak with a foot fetish.

He slid a stool over in front of Sally and sat on it. "The shoes will be right out."

"It's nice to hear you speaking in complete sentences for a change. I was beginning to think that grunting was a new language."

Roger grunted and Sally laughed.

"You're laughing at me?" he asked.

She shrugged. "Sorry. I don't know. I guess you surprised me today."

Jeffrey peeked his head out of the stockroom. "I don't see a size six."

"Check behind the sevens," Roger said. "I had to rearrange some things after the shipment yesterday."

"Gotcha!" Jeffrey disappeared again.

Roger wanted to know how he surprised her but that would require asking a question, which would require speaking. And he'd already spoken enough for one day.

"I saw you go behind the gas station," said Sally. "I know what you did."

Damn.

He didn't want anyone to know about that. He gave her

the silent treatment. It had worked wonders in the past.

Jeffrey approached with the box of shoes and handed them to Roger. "Size six. You're right—they were hidden behind the sevens."

"Thank you," said Roger, pulling the shoes from the box. He removed the paper from the inside of each one and placed the paper in the box. He grabbed one of her feet to slide the shoe on.

Absolutely beautiful feet.

"Ouch," Sally said. "I have a cramp in my foot."

"Where?" asked Roger. He moved his hand to the middle of her arch. "Here?"

"Yes! There, there, there."

Roger worked on her arch with both of his thumbs, pressing, caressing. There's nothing worse than a foot cramp and he hated to see that look of excruciating pain on Sally's face.

Sally closed her eyes and moaned. "Yes. That's it. Right there."

Roger worked the area a little more. "Better?"

"Much. *Thank* you."

"Good. And just so the other foot isn't jealous or decides to have a cramp of its own." He grabbed her other foot and gave it a quick massage with his thumbs. He didn't hear a peep from Sally, so he looked up and her mouth was open. He couldn't get a read on her. Not good. He glanced down at her foot that was still in his hand and he dropped it. "Right.

Okay, let's try on these shoes."

What the hell had happened there? He'd been lost in the world of Sally's feet and time had stood still. He felt drunk. For a brief moment there he didn't have a care in the world. His mind wasn't on anything going on in the world of Roger Hudson and he wasn't obsessing on anything from the past. Amazing. And scary.

Shake it off.

Roger carefully slid the shoe on to her foot, then the second shoe. "There you go. Walk around a little bit and see how that feels. Take your time."

Sally did a few circles in the store, occasionally looking at her feet. She appeared to be deep in thought. She must have been mentally checking her calendar to find the next open spot for a free foot massage from Roger.

What the hell were you thinking?

"You're right." Sally smiled. "These are amazing—so comfy."

"They developed the technology for these shoes at Stanford. They absorb shock and even reduce stress and impact on the knees."

Sally continued to walk around the store in the shoes.

She seemed so different at the moment. Maybe it was the environment since Roger was on home turf, but he felt more comfortable in her presence. Odd. She even seemed . . . tolerable. Almost nice. She must have drugged him. That's gotta be it. Or he got food poisoning and was now delirious.

One of those two, for sure. Whatever the reason, for a brief moment he had considered asking Sally to be his agent.

Pull yourself together! This is the annoying woman who drives you nuts!

Roger's thoughts flashed back to the day before and the agent interviews at Big Basin Homes. What a waste of time that was. He needed to sell his house quick. He wasn't going to live next door to some billionaire who was going to throw loud, extravagant parties and ruin his peaceful neighborhood.

Sally returned to the chair and sat. "These are great. I'll take them."

"Of course," said Roger. "Let me just . . ." He slid the shoes off her feet, careful not to gawk or feel this time, and placed them back in the box. She slipped on her old shoes and followed him to the register.

Jeffrey stepped aside with his notepad and let Roger ring up the purchase.

"Studying?" asked Sally, eyeing Jeffrey's notepad.

"I'm a behavioral neuroscience major," said Jeffrey. "I'm studying my Uncle Roger's——"

Roger cleared his throat. "That'll be $84.75."

"Oh . . ." Sally smiled and pulled her wallet from her purse.

Roger didn't mind helping Jeffrey with his studies, but Sally didn't need to know he was being put under the microscope by his nephew. He tapped Jeffrey on the side of the arm and gestured with his thumb toward the stockroom. Jeffrey winked and disappeared behind the curtain.

Sally shuffled through the credit card section of her wallet and sighed. "That's weird—the credit card isn't where I usually keep it. I just used it at Highway 9—maybe it fell out." She set the wallet on the counter and pulled items out of her large purse, one at a time. Lip gloss. Cell phone. Sunglasses. Hand sanitizer. Plastic bag with pistachios. Pack of gum. Small pack of tissues. Keychain. Calculator. Business cards.

"Is that a bottomless purse?" asked Roger.

Sally laughed and continued her search. It was so odd he wasn't annoyed with her at the moment. And she smelled fantastic. Roger grabbed one of her business cards and examined it, his eyes immediately drawn to the photo on the left. He glanced up at her again. She had a beautiful smile in the photo, but she was much prettier in person.

"Found it!" she said, handing Roger her credit card.

Damn.

Sally saw him stick her business card in the drawer. He pulled the card back out of the drawer and placed it back on the counter. "Sorry. I shouldn't have assumed I could take one."

"No, no, no. Of course you can have a card." She slid the business card back in his direction. "But I thought you had an agent since you were interviewing yesterday."

He tore the receipt from the machine and passed it to

her with a pen. "Not even close. You work with a bunch of imbeciles over there, you know that?"

"Well," she said, signing the receipt and sliding it back to him. "You just haven't found the right one yet, that's all. There are plenty of wonderful agents in the area. I'm sure you'll find one soon."

He was so tempted to just hire her. He needed to sell his house!

Sally lunged for the pen as it rolled toward the edge of the counter. Roger reached out at the same time, his hand landing on top of hers.

As wonderful and soft as her hand felt, it was awkward.

Say something.

"Paper," he said, removing his hand from the top of hers.

"Pardon me?"

"Paper, rock, scissors? Or is it rock, paper, scissors?"

Sally smiled. "I was never good at that game." She gathered her things from the counter and placed them back in her purse. She opened the lip gloss and slid it across her lips.

She had nice lips. Kissable. He looked away. It had been so long since his last kiss he couldn't even remember what it felt like. He pretended to arrange some papers under the cash register to get distracted.

Hire her. No, don't do it. Do it, you bozo.

"Roger?"

"You're hired!" he said, a little louder than expected.

Crouton popped out of his bed, ready to defend the store. "Arf! Arf! Arf!"

"Calm down, Crouton. Everything is okay." Roger reached down and scratched him on the top of his head. Roger pointed to an area a few feet from where he and Sally were standing. "You may want to move quickly over to that space over there. Crouton tends to be a little gassy when he's scared."

Sally laughed and took a few steps back. "Okay."

She stood there staring at Roger for what seemed like days. Roger fidgeted and wondered what she was waiting for.

Did I forget to give her the credit card back? He glanced down at the counter. Nothing.

"My shoes?" she said.

"Oh! Of course."

What an idiot.

At least she didn't mention anything about him saying she was hired. What was he thinking? That's just it—he wasn't thinking at all. His mind and body acted in mysterious ways in her presence. What was going on?

Roger came from behind the counter and handed her the bag with her new shoes. "Here you go. Thanks for stopping by."

"Thank you," she said. "Enjoy the rest of your day." She turned to leave and then stopped, turning back around.

"Oh . . . you mentioned I was hired."

"Did I?"

"Yeah. Right before Crouton had his little episode of gas."

Roger nodded. "Oh, that. Right. Well, I need to sell my house right away. I've heard you're good at what you do, but you're probably too busy. Forget I even mentioned it. Have a great—"

"I'd be happy to sell your house for you."

"Oh . . ." Roger was relieved and scared at the same time. "You sure?"

Sally laughed. "I guess the question should be if *you're* sure."

Do it. Say yes. Don't be an idiot. The sooner you sell the house the better.

"Okay," said Roger. "Let's do it."

"Great!" said Sally. "I can stop by this evening and I'll do a comparative market analysis on your home, if that works for you."

"Of course."

Roger gave her his address and they agreed she would stop by later in the evening at seven. He couldn't believe it. He was going to hire the most annoying woman in the world. But for some reason he felt confident she would sell his house quickly and that's what mattered most.

Jeffrey came out of the stockroom after she left, grinning. "Very, very interesting."

Roger opened the drawer and placed the receipt from Sally's purchase in the receipt envelope. "What are you talking about?"

"You and Sally. I wish I could have videotaped that. It was fascinating and very telling. There's something going on between you two—I can feel it."

"Right . . ."

"Seriously. The interaction between you two, as stilted and awkward as it was, was like you were on a blind date. And the way you looked at her when she wasn't looking and the way she was checking you out when you weren't watching was amazing! The eyes tell everything."

"She was checking me out?"

"Big time."

His nephew must have been high. That would explain the nonsense coming out of his mouth.

Roger glared at Jeffrey. "And what are my eyes telling you right now?"

"That I should drop the subject."

"Smart boy."

Jeffrey wrote a few more notes and chuckled.

"What now?" said Roger. "What did you just write?"

"Insecure, are we? I should jot that down, too."

"Tell me."

Jeffrey laughed and flipped his notebook around so Roger could read it. Roger's eyes dropped to the very last thing written on the page in large letters.

Roger and Sally will be married within six months.

Roger shook his head in disgust. "My poor, delusional nephew. I should be studying *you*."

"Six months. Mark my words. I've learned a lot over the last few years and my professor says I have a keen sense of awareness and observation. He has no doubts I'm going to graduate at the top of my class."

"You may just do that, but you're still living in a fantasy world when it comes to me and Sally."

"You wanna bet?"

"That Sally and I will be married within six months?"

"Yup. How about a hundred dollars?"

"Easy for you to say since you're betting with money you don't have. But don't you worry—I can take it out of your paycheck." He shook Jeffrey's hand. "You're on."

Jeffrey's prediction was crazy. Yes, he thought Sally was attractive and, yes, he had felt some odd sensations in her presence. That was it! The plan was to use her real estate services. Nothing more. In fact, it was time to get her out of his head until they met later for business. He had work to do. He headed back to the stockroom and tried to rearrange the new shoes so everything was organized again. He set a couple of boxes on the floor, reached for a box and stared at it for a moment. Size six. Sally's size.

Damn.

His thoughts returned to her shapely legs which were connected to the most amazing feet. He enjoyed giving her that foot massage. A little too much.

Not good.

The door swung open again.

Roger rubbed his forehead. "Geez, Louise."

The Mouth had returned.

"Good boy!" said Maggie, approaching Roger. "I just heard you hired Sally to be your agent."

Why wasn't he surprised she already knew?

Roger bent down below the counter and adjusted the stack of paper shopping bags.

Maggie squatted to pet Crouton on the head. "Sally is the best in the business, you'll love her. Just wanted to say congratulations and remind you she's single. Oh! And you may want to consider buying William and Tammy Fusco's home since they're going to sell it. It's *wonder*ful."

Roger popped back up from below the counter. "The Fuscos are selling their home? Since when?"

William and Tammy had an amazing property on Yuba Court. Roger used to deliver newspapers there as a kid. They had a magnolia tree in their front yard even more mature than his.

Maggie picked up the violet suede Prada almond toe pump from the display and smelled it. "They bought a home in Palm Springs and they'll be leaving soon. How do you *not* know this? Are you a hermit? William says the retirement community down there is incredible and there are a thousand golf courses, but I know the real reason he's moving."

"Good for you. I don't need to know."

Maggie placed the Prada pump back where she found it. "Yes, you do want to know. Rumor has it he's an undercover agent for the—"

Roger cleared his throat. "Can we get back to the topic of their house? How long has the house been on the market?"

"Oh, it's not for sale yet. They have to do upgrades before they sell it."

This was great news and Roger needed to mention this to Sally when he saw her.

He wanted that house and she was going to help him get it.

Chapter Five

At ten minutes before seven Sally pulled up to Roger's home, located on a quiet, tree-lined street just around the corner from West Valley College. She turned off the ignition and stared through the window at his lovely four bedroom, three bath home with the three-car garage. The front of the house was lined with bright red bricks and the front door was stunning between the tall white columns.

Sally loved the large magnolia tree out front in the middle of the lawn. The swing that hung from one of the large limbs put an instant smile on her face and flashed her back to her childhood. It reminded her of the Fuscos' house. She was curious about the swing. If Sally had to guess, she would say Roger was around sixty years old so the swing didn't make much sense at all.

The yard was very well manicured. It was obvious Roger had a gardener come to keep things looking nice. If the inside was as well kept as the outside, she was confident she could sell this house the first weekend. Houses in this area didn't last long on the market and that was a good thing.

Sally grabbed her briefcase from the back seat of her car and walked up the path to the front door. Before she could ring the bell the door opened.

"Good evening," said Roger, very business-like.

"Good evening, Roger," said Sally, matching his tone but smiling.

She eyed his casual clothes. She'd always seen him wearing suits at Highway 9, so this was a surprise, to say the least. He wore jeans that fit him well. His black polo shirt matched his salt and pepper hair and hugged his upper body, showing off his chest and toned arms. His casual black leather shoes looked comfortable, like they were made more for walking. Roger Hudson was a good-looking man and in excellent shape for his age. Heck, he'd be considered in great shape at any age.

"And thank you for being on time," Roger said. He eyed her car on the street. "Audi A4. Nice car. I like the red."

"Thank you." Sally turned around and pointed toward the magnolia tree. "I love the swing."

"I hung it for the neighborhood children. I got the idea from someone else. The kids come around every now and then and use it—they seem to get a kick out of it." He waved Sally inside. "Please."

"Of course."

Sally took another look back at the swing before she entered. Another surprise about Roger. It was interesting that he said he had hung it for the neighborhood kids. He didn't have kids of his own? Surely if he had had kids they would have been in their thirties by now.

Roger closed the door behind them and she followed him through the formal tiled entry into the back of the house. They stopped in a large open area that was the kitchen and family room combined. The house was like a showroom: clean, clutter-free, very well organized. She couldn't have staged the home any better if she'd tried.

Jeffrey entered through the sliding door from the backyard and waved. "Hi, Sally." He wore khaki shorts and a t-shirt with an Aztec warrior and the letters SDSU on the chest.

"Hi, Jeffrey," she replied. "Nice to see you."

Jeffrey continued to the kitchen and sat on one of the stools, opening up his notebook.

"Can I get you something to drink?" asked Roger. "Water, coffee, tea, carrot juice . . ."

"No, thanks."

". . . orange juice, pineapple juice, milk."

"I'm fine."

"Beer, wine . . ."

Sally laughed. "I haven't eaten so just the smell of beer or wine would get me drunk."

"Is that a yes or a no?"

"No, thank you."

"Very interesting," said Jeffrey. He wrote something in his notebook.

Roger gave Jeffrey a look and he winked back at his uncle.

Sally glanced around the house and nodded her approval. "Your home is amazing. Looks like the shoe business has been *very* good to you."

"Yes and no. The business has been great, no doubt. But I did need help from an inheritance to be able to acquire this house. That's also how I was able to get out of selling shoes at Nordstrom and open my own store."

She spotted a dog bed on the floor in front of the fireplace and another one in the kitchen near the kitchen island next to Jeffrey. "And where is little Crouton?"

Roger pointed down the hallway. "He's sleeping on my bed, which unfortunately he thinks is *his* bed." Roger whistled. "Crouton! Come! Intruder!"

Crouton came jamming around the corner from the master bedroom to the family room, grunting with each step. She wondered if Crouton had learned the grunting from Roger or the other way around.

"Get her, Crouton," said Roger. "Let her have it."

"Arf! Arf!"

Crouton screeched to a halt in front of Sally and licked her feet through the open-toed shoes.

Sally laughed and bent down to stroke the dog as he continued to lick her feet. "Hello, Crouton, you sweet little thing." She stood up and glanced at Roger, who was still looking at her feet.

Odd.

She cleared her throat. "Do you have a cleaning service

that comes in?"

Roger broke his gaze away from her feet and huffed. "Why would I pay someone to do what I could do with my own two hands?"

Crouton finished with Sally's feet and plopped down on his bed in front of the fireplace.

She peeked into the backyard and admired the dark green lawn and a fountain in the middle. "And the yard?"

Roger followed her eyes to the backyard. "What about it?"

"It's immaculate. Do you have a gardening service that takes care of that?"

He huffed again and stuck his chest out. "What do you take me for? A lazy ass?"

Jeffrey wrote a few more notes.

Great job, Sally. Pissing off the client before he signs the contract.

"No, not at all," she said. "It's just . . . the yard is a-*mazing!* The front yard, too. And with you owning a business I just assumed you didn't have time to do so many things at home as well."

Good save.

"I love my business but it isn't my life. I'm more of a homebody and I like things to be neat and orderly. Yes, it takes time but I don't mind at all. Plus, it helps keep my mind off of —" He stared at Sally for a moment, looking like he had said too much. "Anyway, let's get started."

"Of course."

It definitely looked like she touched a nerve but it was time to move on and get down to business. "I start off by giving you a CMA—a comparative market analysis. I'll need to look at the entire house, including the garage. I'll take notes, do some research, and then give you my suggestions for putting the home up for sale. It's an easy process."

"Take a look around. Let me know if you need anything in the meantime."

Sally smiled. "Actually, if you can show me around that would make it easier in case I have questions." She opened her briefcase and pulled out a folder. Then she grabbed a pen and turned to him.

He hesitated for a moment. "Okay." He led Sally down the hallway; the first stop was his office. Jeffrey followed closely with his notebook.

Sally entered the office, flipped open the folder, and wrote a few notes. She opened the closet door, peeked inside, and then shut the door. "Beautiful office. I love the desk. Walnut?"

"Yes," said Roger.

They went through the two bedrooms before ending up in the master suite at the end of the hallway. Another spotless room. The cherry wood headboard matched the two night stands and dresser. She quickly eyed the photo on top of the dresser. Roger was by the ocean with a beautiful brunette.

His wife.

She smiled at the green comforter with the tulips. Obviously chosen by his wife.

"Have you done any improvements to the house recently?" asked Sally.

"How recently are you talking about?"

"I don't know. Let's go back five years."

Roger stared at her for a moment. "Let's not."

"Pardon me?"

Damn it all. Roger hadn't thought this through very well. He certainly didn't want the subject of Macy coming up. Sally had glanced at the photo on the dresser and he was glad she didn't ask about it. And now that he had thought about it, he'd be selling his house five years after she had died.

Some tribute.

Roger sat on the bed, feeling guilty. Right on cue, as if the dumb dog could sense Roger's mood change, Crouton sprinted into the room and leaped from the floor to the bed. He cuddled up against Roger.

"Amazing!" said Sally. "I had no idea pugs could jump so high. He's the Michael Jordan of dogs!"

"Yeah." Roger rubbed Crouton under his chin and forced a smile. Man, he felt pathetic in front of Sally.

Thankfully, Jeffrey jumped in and saved him, pointing to

the master bathroom. "This bathroom was completely remodeled five years ago. Actually all three bathrooms were, along with the kitchen."

Sally took some notes. "This is great. Okay, we're done in here. Just a bit more and I'll be out of your hair."

Thank you!

She probably took pity on Roger.

Back in the family room Sally pointed to the multi-colored stones on the fireplace. She knew it wasn't the original. "When was the fireplace redone?"

"Also five years ago," said Jeffrey.

Roger turned to his nephew. "I can take over from here."

"Sounds good," said Jeffrey, stepping back and taking notes. In fact, his nephew was taking more notes than Sally! He needed to ask Jeffrey about them later. Either that or he'd steal them and run them through the shredder.

Sally eyed the picture on the mantle and looked away. Another photo with Macy, this one taken in Golden Gate Park. He needed to say something instead of being such a pathetic human being.

Just do it. Get it over with.

Roger pointed to the photo. "My wife Macy. She died five years ago. Cancer."

"I'm sorry." She glanced back at the photo. "She's beautiful."

Roger nodded.

Jeffrey stepped forward. "Aunt Macy was one of the

kindest women I knew. She was always giving to others—especially the homeless."

Sally turned and locked eyes with Roger. "That's wonderful. We need more people like her in the world." She gave Roger a smile and sighed. "Okay, I need to see the garage."

"Is that necessary?" asked Roger.

"Absolutely necessary. Why?"

Roger didn't answer.

Sally nodded. "I think I know what's going on here. Your house is spotless inside because you crammed everything into the garage."

Jeffrey laughed. "Not quite. But you should brace yourself—it's something like you've never seen."

Sally waved Jeffrey's comments off. "Believe me, I've seen it all. Is it a man cave filled with every possible tool and gadget? Seen that too many times to count."

"You've never seen *this* before."

"Color me intrigued. Let's go."

Great. What will she think? The only other person who had been inside that garage in the last five years other than Roger had been Jeffrey.

Roger led the way to the garage, pulled the door open, and waved Sally and Jeffrey through.

Sally stepped down two steps and stopped. "I can't see anything."

Roger clicked on the lights.

Sally raised her hand to her chest. "Oh my . . ."

Roger pictured her mouth open but he wasn't certain since she stood directly in front of him. He took a moment to drop his gaze down to her legs.

Those legs will be the death of me.

Sally turned around and Roger's eyes shot back to meet hers.

"This is so amazing," she said. "I guess I *haven't* seen everything."

It was Roger's getaway. His place to disconnect and forget about life for a while.

Sally's eyes traveled around his garage that had been converted into a vintage movie theater. Velvet curtains lined the side walls and the ceiling was art deco. There was even a counter with a bright red and yellow antique corn popper, a soda fountain, and a glass display with candy. The seating was for eight people and the vintage chairs were customized with a few modern conveniences.

Sally pointed to the seat that was front and center. "May I?"

"Of course," said Roger.

She sat and kicked off her shoes, reclining in the leather chair. Roger leaned forward to take a peek at her feet but the lighting wasn't the greatest. Sally ran her hands along the arms of the chair and over the drink cup holder. She stopped when she noticed the button on the right arm of the chair. "What's this button for?"

"Press it," said Jeffrey.

Sally pressed the button and a moment later a smile formed on her face. "Lumbar support!" She let out a deep breath. "I'm speechless."

Impossible.

She twisted around so she could look at Roger. "What kind of movies do you watch?"

"Only the classics," he answered. "*Casablanca. Gone With The Wind. A Streetcar Named Desire*. Are we done here?"

"I love them all except the last one. Never heard of it."

"The last one was a question. Are we done here?"

Sally popped up out of the seat and laughed. "Oh! Sorry." She slipped her shoes back on and walked back around the theater seats, standing in front of Roger and Jeffrey. Then she frowned.

"What's wrong?" asked Roger.

She crinkled her nose. "This is the most amazing theater, but I'm not sure how appealing it'll be to potential buyers. Most people in this area have children and they need the space in their garages for the cars and storage."

Roger gestured around the theater. "Oh, this isn't staying."

"It's not?"

"Of course not. I'm taking it with me to the new house."

"I'm sorry. I wasn't aware there was a new house."

"Not yet. You're going to help me find one, aren't you?"

Sally smiled. "Of course!"

"In fact, I'd like you to find out what's happening with William and Tammy Fusco's property on Yuba Court. I hear they're moving."

Sally's head jerked back.

Roger took a step closer. "Are you okay? You look like you're going to pass out."

"Fine, fine. Just a sharp pain but it went away." She rubbed her forehead. "How did you hear about their house?"

"Well, I've always known about their home. That's where I got the swing idea from. But *Maggie* is the one who told me they were going to sell their place and it's in the perfect location. I remember how picky the Fuscos were when they came in for shoes, so I'm guessing they keep their place immaculate. Can you get in touch with them and arrange a visit? If we get lucky we can negotiate something before it even hits the market."

"You know . . . I'm not sure that house is the right one for you."

"Why is that?"

"I think it's pretty small compared to your place here."

"I thought it was bigger."

Sally blinked a couple of times. "Tell you what . . . let me pull up some info on their house from the MLS system and I can share it with you later. Then we can figure out for sure if it's everything you're looking for. How's that?"

"Great idea. I'm *very* interested."

Sally explained to Roger that they would meet the next day after lunch and she'd present him with the Comparative Market Analysis. All she needed to do was take pictures of the house and have him sign the listing agreement. Then she'd put the house on the market and arrange an open house for the weekend.

"I should be able to sell your home rather quickly," she said. "It's in great shape."

"That's exactly what I wanted to hear."

Ideally, he'd like to be out before they started the demolition next door.

Sally clapped her hands once. "We're done then!"

Roger pushed the door open and held it there with his arm for Sally as she slid sideways past him. It was a tight squeeze and they brushed bodies.

Jeffrey winked at his uncle as he slid by. He stopped and leaned in, pretending to smell Roger's neck. "You smell nice."

"Move it or lose it."

After Sally left Jeffrey approached Roger in the kitchen. "Remember what I wrote yesterday? I changed my mind."

"Good to hear it. But you're not getting out of our bet."

"Now why would I want to do that?" Jeffrey held the notepad to Roger's face.

Roger and Sally will be married within ~~six~~ three months.

Roger sighed. "If you want to live to see tomorrow, you'd better sleep with one eye open tonight."

"You know I'm right. In fact, I'd be more than happy to double our wager."

"Two hundred bucks?"

"Two hundred. You'll be married within three months. I'm sure of it."

"More like full of it." Roger shook his hand. "I'll take that bet. Sucker."

Jeffrey laughed. "We'll see who the sucker is soon."

Roger didn't like how confident Jeffrey was. Could his nephew see something he couldn't see?

Nah. No way.

Chapter Six

The next day at lunch Roger sat at his usual table at Highway 9 Sandwiches with his tuna sandwich. He looked forward to meeting with Sally afterward to get his house on the market. The woman had to eat, though, so he knew it would only be a matter of time before she showed up and ordered her ham and Swiss—

"What a beautiful day!" Sally yelled.

She startled Roger, causing him to crush the drink cup in his hand. The lid popped off and root beer shot across the table and onto his sandwich. "Geez, Louise!" He jumped up before the root beer dripped off the table and onto his slacks. "Do you have a volume button?" He reached for some napkins and patted the puddles on the table. "Mute would be even better. And what makes this day so beautiful, anyway?"

Sally smiled. "Every day is beautiful." She glanced down at his sandwich and frowned. "Sorry about that. I can buy you another one."

"No."

"Then think of it like a root beer float. But instead of ice cream floating, it's your sandwich. Kind of funny."

He blinked. "Don't you have a ham and Swiss to

purchase?"

"Yes! Be right back."

Sally slid by Roger in her short black pencil skirt and white blouse. Roger would guess they called that business casual but he called it a complete distraction. He tried to resist her legs this time but it was no use. He sneaked a peek and continued eating his now-soggy sandwich.

Five minutes later Sally came out of the sandwich shop and pulled out the chair directly next to Roger at his table.

What the hell is this crazy woman doing?

He reached out and stopped the backward motion of the chair with his hand. Just because he chose her to be his real estate agent didn't make them buddies. She could go sit at another table.

She smiled and tried to pull the chair but he had it locked in place—it wasn't going anywhere.

"Okay." She let go of the chair. "But I just figured we should sit together and talk business while we ate."

"You figured wrong." He could feel her staring at him. He pointed across the way. "Your usual table is available with a *beautiful* view of the asphalt. I like to use a lot of space when I eat. You know . . . just in case someone wants to scare the crap out of me by yelling something ridiculous about the weather."

He took another bite of his soggy sandwich and grimaced.

Sally sat at the other table. "As you wish. I was just trying to be sociable."

There's that word again. Sociable. What did Jeffrey call him? Antisocial? Or was it unsociable? He couldn't remember and it didn't matter. As far as he was concerned his relationship with Sally was strictly business. She had the best set of legs west of the Mississippi, but that wasn't enough to motivate him to engage in daily chit chat with her.

As if she were reading his mind and trying to torture him, Sally crossed her legs and her skirt slid up her thigh a little. Roger took a deep breath and kept his eyes focused on his sandwich.

Tempting, but you're strong.

He took another bite and spit it out into the sandwich basket. "What the hell am I doing? This is disgusting."

"It can't be that bad," said Sally, working on her dry sandwich.

Roger held out his sandwich. "You want a bite?" A few drops of root beer dripped from the bread to the ground.

"Thanks, but I'm very happy with mine."

"I'll bet you are. I'll see you in your office in one hour." He stood and held out his hand. "Can I get the other half of your sandwich before I go?"

Sally stared down at her sandwich and she continued to chew. "My other half?"

"You never eat it. And why is that, anyway? You shouldn't waste food."

She looked at her sandwich again. "It's my favorite

sandwich but it's too big and they don't offer a smaller size."

His hand still waited for it.

Sally glanced down the street toward the gas station. "Are you going to take it over to the——"

"Does it matter?"

She shook her head. "No. It doesn't." She wrapped up the other half of the sandwich neatly and handed it to him. "You don't fool me, Roger Hudson."

He took the sandwich from her. "What are you talking about?"

"You have a crusty exterior like apple pie. But you're also just as sweet."

Roger grunted. "I'm not sweet. I'm humane. There's a big difference."

Forty-five minutes after lunch, Sally was in her office organizing the file for Roger Hudson. After he had left Highway 9 Sandwiches, she watched him walk down the street behind the gas station to give the rest of her sandwich to that homeless man again. His kindness touched her heart. What didn't make sense was why he was so uptight with her today. He seemed to have lost a little bit of his edge last night when she had visited his home but his bitterness had returned today full force. Still, she was grateful to have him as a client and looked forward to selling his home. Then she would buy the Fuscos' house. Of course there was that tiny problem of Roger expressing an interest in the same property. She should tell him she *really* wanted the house, so he could focus on others. But what if he didn't care? What if he still had an interest in the Fuscos' house? He surely had more money than she did and could easily outbid her. Then there would be that other issue of conflict of interest.

"Hey," said Portia, peeking her head into Sally's office. "Busy?"

Sally set Roger's file aside. "No. I'm just getting Roger Hudson's CMA together and going over the contract before he arrives."

Portia sat down in the chair in front of Sally's desk. "Mr. Crotchety is coming back? Oh, joy."

"Shhh!" Sally glanced behind Portia to make sure there wasn't anybody within hearing distance. Especially Roger. "He's going to be here any minute, so keep it down. And he's not as bad as people think, so be nice."

"Ha! During the agent interviews he told John he smelled like a rotten rat and that there was no way in hell he wanted a smelly real estate agent."

Sally laughed. "Would you want a smelly agent?"

Portia laughed. "Okay, maybe not. I'll give him that one. But he did dismiss me immediately because I was fifteen minutes late after coming from a lunch with a client. He wouldn't even let me explain that my client's car broke down and I offered to drive her home, which was not on the way here. Anyway, I guess he was meant to be your client, so that's what counts. I would've strangled him anyway. Why do you have that grin on your face?"

"I always have a grin on my face."

"This one's different."

"I don't think so!" said Sally, laughing.

She knows me so well.

Portia wagged a finger at Sally. "Spill it."

"Seriously, he's not such a bad guy. I've learned a lot about that man and remember, he's been through a lot."

"You *like* him?"

"I'm just saying I think he's an okay guy and—"

"Do you find him attractive?"

Sally sighed. "Are you seriously asking me this?"

Portia crossed her arms. "Yes or no?"

She threw her palms in the air. "Anyone can see Roger Hudson is a sexy man."

Sally froze.

Portia scooted to the edge of the chair. "Why are you looking at me that way? Are you breathing? Are you choking on your own saliva? You're turning red."

Sally shuffled papers on her desk. A paper clip fell off the desk and she reached for it. Then she banged her head on the open drawer on the way back up.

"Ouch!" she said, rubbing her head.

Portia's eyes grew wider. She leaned in and whispered. "Is Roger behind us?"

Sally nodded and forced a smile.

Portia swung around in her chair and stared at Roger on the other side of the glass with his arms folded.

Sally jumped up and waved him in like she hadn't seen him there. "Come in!"

Portia stood and crossed paths with Roger as she headed out of Sally's office. She checked her watch and gave Roger a tsk tsk. "You're late. You may want to work on that."

Sally let out a nervous laugh. "She's kidding." She pointed to the chair. "Please have a seat and we can get started."

Roger sat in the chair and cleared his throat. "I was out in the lobby and the receptionist said I could come back. Sorry to interrupt your . . . conversation."

He heard us for sure.

Sally touched her face—it burned. Her client heard her say she thought he was a sexy man.

Forget about it. Get to work.

Sally tried to calm her mind and get her heart rate down to sub-hummingbird levels. She went over the home analysis with Roger and he signed the contract for the listing.

"The goal is to get your home into the MLS system this evening and ready for sale tomorrow. Then I'll have an open house this Saturday and Sunday."

"Perfect. Anything else?"

She shook her head. "I just need to take some pictures of your home."

"I have to get back to the store and do some inventory now. I made a copy of the key to my house for you." He stood and pulled his keychain from his pocket. He removed one of the keys from the key ring and handed it to her. "Let yourself in and do whatever you need to do."

"Great! I think we're done for now."

Her eyes were drawn toward his hands as he fidgeted with his keychain.

Those wonderful hands.

Roger had given Sally one of the best foot massages ever and she'd kill to have another one.

Would it be bad to fake a foot cramp?

Twenty minutes later Sally took pictures of Roger's home. Without him. It felt kind of weird, considering her clients were usually with her when she shot the photos. But she liked that he was just as anxious and motivated as she was to sell the house.

After the exterior shots she went inside and shot pictures of the master bedroom. She entered the walk-in closet and stopped. There was a small box on the floor with MACY written on top. She stared at the box for a moment, curious what was inside. Jewelry? Pictures? Ashes? She wasn't the kind of person who would snoop into other people's belongings. Just in case, she needed to leave the closet before she did something stupid. It did give her the urge to look at the photo on the night stand again. She picked up the picture frame and looked a little closer. They looked happy in the picture. Roger was a different man—his smile so pure and sincere, like he was head over heels in love.

She placed the picture frame back in its place and took pictures of the rest of the house. The place was amazing. Why did he want to move? Too many memories? Time for a new chapter in his life? She wanted to know more about Roger, but for now it was time to go. She walked down the hallway and stopped at the door that led to the garage.

The theater.

She had never encountered anything like that before in her career. Sure, some of her clients had home theaters, but usually they were in converted bedrooms or basements. Roger's theater was amazing.

Just a quick look.

Sally opened the door to the garage, flipped on the light, and stepped down into the theater.

She sighed. "I want a theater like this."

She eyed the vintage poster of the movie *Roman Holiday*. She smiled and glanced over at the counter. In the glass display case was a box of Red Vines.

I love those.

Next to the Red Vines was a box of chocolate-covered raisins.

Love those too.

Who was she kidding? Sally had a sweet tooth and loved just about everything.

She sat in the first theater chair and reclined it back.

"This feels nice. Okay, start the movie!"

She pictured *Roman Holiday* or one of the other classics Roger loved coming on. How funny that the cranky man was a romantic.

Sally heard a noise inside the house and a few seconds later the pitter patter of dog feet.

"Arf! Arf!"

Crouton appeared below her. The dog smiled and wagged his little curly tail.

This can't be happening.

If Crouton was there that meant Roger was there. And she was lounging in one of his chairs.

She grabbed the lever to put the recliner back to its default position. The leg rest lowered over Crouton's head and pushed the dog directly under the chair.

"Oh, no!"

Crouton was trapped underneath the chair and all Sally could hear was muffled barks.

"Hang on, Crouton!"

"Arf! Arf! Arf!"

Sally grabbed the lever but was afraid she was going to hurt Crouton. She didn't know what to do.

Jeffrey ran into the garage and stopped in front of Sally. "What happened?"

"Crouton is trapped inside this chair! I reclined it back down and it swept him underneath!"

Jeffrey laughed. "Okay, no problem. You think this is the first time? Hang on." Jeffrey stood behind the chair and pushed the top of the back forward. The bottom opened up underneath and Crouton popped out.

"Arf! Arf!"

"Oh, thank God." She reached down, picked up Crouton and was greeted with licks. Sally laughed but she really wanted to cry. That was so scary and she hadn't known what to do. She turned to Jeffrey. "Thank you so much. That would've been horrible if anything had happened to him."

Jeffrey reached over and petted Crouton on the head. "He always gets into things—this is nothing new."

"He's just the cutest dog. How did he get his name?"

"Ahh." Jeffrey scratched the side of his face. "It's a beautiful story. Uncle Roger and Aunt Macy met in the supermarket—they both were reaching for the last bag of croutons. She let him have the bag even though he insisted that she take it. So, they hit it off and later got married. She had always wanted a pug but they weren't home much, so it didn't make much sense to get a dog. Later when she was sick, toward the end, he got Crouton for her. He told her he would always remember the croutons she let him have on that wonderful day they met and he wanted to return the favor."

Sally felt her eyes sting. "That's very sweet."

"Don't let his bitter facade fool you. He's a good man. I personally think he's over Aunt Macy's death, but he's just used to being crabby. It's like his newly found comfort zone, a shield for him."

"It must have been a difficult time."

"It was very hard on the entire family. I still can't believe she's gone. But it was especially hard on Roger. He was madly in love with Aunt Macy. They were inseparable."

Sally smiled. "He'll get through it."

"To tell you the truth, I think you've been helping him."

"Me?" She chuckled. "I doubt that."

"Believe me, I can see it. He's been softening lately. Little by little, he'll get back to his old self. Have patience with him and know that if he says something harsh, he doesn't mean it."

Sally smiled. "Sounds good. Well, I should get going. Do we need to tell Roger I almost crushed his dog?"

Jeffrey grabbed Crouton from Sally and laughed. "It will be our little secret. And if it will make you feel better, you can ask my uncle about the time Crouton jumped in the dryer."

"No! Roger didn't turn it on, did he?"

"No."

"Thank goodness."

Jeffrey walked Sally out to her car. She placed the camera in her purse and dropped it on the back seat. Then she turned to Jeffrey. "I'll send Roger an email later."

"Sounds good."

"Before I go, can ask you something?"

"Of course. Anything."

"Why is he selling the house? We never discussed it and it's such an amazing place."

Jeffrey pointed to the house next door. "Some guy bought that place and is going to tear it down to build a mansion. Uncle Roger doesn't want to live next to somebody like that. The guy is going to have ten bedrooms and he's single. Go figure. Uncle Roger doesn't like to see waste."

"Of course. Makes sense."

Thinking of her sandwiches at lunch, Sally felt guilty on the drive back home. She wasn't wasting the food on purpose. They were her favorite sandwiches in the world, but they were so big! They didn't taste the same when they were cold or reheated and that was the only reason why she didn't eat all of it. Roger was kind to care about people he didn't know. To take the time to make sure someone else had something to eat.

The more she got to know about Roger, the more she liked him. But she wasn't going to make him her project and try to change him. He would change on his own time—when he was ready—and travel down the road of happiness again. Sally didn't believe a person only had one shot at love. She had hope for herself. She had messed up her marriage by being too obsessed with her career. Never again. She knew what was important in life now. The thought of meeting someone new gave her butterflies. The image of Roger popped into her brain.

She shook her head.

What am I getting myself into?

Chapter Seven

Two days later Sally was ready for Roger's open house. She had placed her real estate signs on the major cross streets in the neighborhood and opened the front door of his house. She was motivated. This house would sell fast.

Thirty seconds later the first car pulled up in front and a family of four got out—a couple, who appeared to be in their thirties with their two toddlers.

"Welcome!" said Sally. She introduced herself and handed the woman a flyer with information about Roger's house. "Let me know if you have any questions."

"Thank you," said the woman, who eyed the flyer and followed her husband down the hallway.

Sally worked on her laptop at the kitchen table while the family toured the home. She could hear them chat and they were impressed so far. This was going to be a great day, Sally could feel it. Who knows, maybe her first visitors would make an offer!

Sally heard another car pull up to the front of the house. *Yes!*

She went to the door to greet the potential buyer and lost her smile.

Roger.

What the heck was he doing here? She specifically gave him instructions to stay away from the open house. The best thing her clients could do for her was let her do her job. They sometimes thought they could help by being there to answer questions about the house, but they always just got in the way. They're not sales people.

She sighed as he approached the front door. "Roger——"

He held up his hand. "Don't get your panties in a bunch. I forgot something and need to grab it out of my office. It'll just be a minute."

"Make it quick."

Roger threw her a military salute and passed by her on the way to the office.

Sally was glad he remembered how she felt about clients being in the home during an open house. She smiled as he disappeared inside his office. A few seconds later he came out and headed to the front door.

"See how fast that was?" Roger said. "In and out."

"Thank you," said Sally. "I appreciate it."

"Look at that," said the man, laughing in the master bedroom. "That's absolutely ridiculous. If we buy this place that would be the first thing to go."

Roger stopped in his tracks and turned his head back toward the master bedroom to listen.

Sally took a few steps forward. "Roger. You were leaving. Remember?"

More laughter from the bedroom.

Roger ignored Sally and walked down the hallway toward his bedroom.

"Roger!" said Sally in a loud whisper. "Come here!"

Sally raced down the hall and tried to grab Roger's arm before he entered the room, but she couldn't get a good grip. She followed Roger into the bedroom and practically ran into his back.

The couple stared up into the skylight and laughed while their two kids pressed their mouths against the sliding glass door that led out to the backyard.

"What's the problem?"

The man turned and raised an eyebrow. "No problem. We were just looking at the skylight."

Sally touched Roger's arm. "Can I speak to you for a moment in the kitchen?"

Roger pointed up at the skylight. "You don't like it?"

The man shook his head. "Not even a tiny bit." He stared back up into it again and laughed. "Why in the world would anybody have a skylight that was the shape of California?"

"It's the shape of a boot, actually."

The man looked up again. "Ah, yeah, I see it now. Even worse."

The kids were now full-on licking the sliding glass door.

Sally glanced at Roger—he looked nauseated. "You okay?" She cleared her throat. "Roger?"

"Lovely," said Roger, pointing to the kids. "*Really* lovely. Especially considering that's the same part of the glass my dog licks every day right after he's done cleaning his privates. In fact, he's even taken a piss on that exact spot a few times. It's a shame I've never had time to clean it."

"Josh! Samantha!" said the woman. "Stop that." She grabbed both children by the hand and led them out of the room. "We're leaving. Now!"

"Bacteria is a nasty thing!" said Roger.

The husband glared at Roger and rushed out of the room.

Sally stood there, speechless. After she heard the front door slam she placed both hands on her hips and turned to Roger. She waited for the stubborn man in front of her to say something. Anything. But he just stood there. Was he waiting for her to speak? Fine.

Sally tried to remain calm. "What on earth were you thinking?"

Roger shrugged. "Smudge marks make me twitchy."

"Twitchy . . ."

"There was no way I was going to sell my house to those idiots. Did you see those kids of theirs? Savages. They'd tear this place apart."

"Why do you care? You won't even be here. You don't have to deal with those kids."

"It doesn't matter. I want my house to go to someone who deserves it. Who appreciates it. They laughed at the

84

skylight—that was my wife's idea! I love that skylight! And they want to rip it out? Hell, no. Not gonna happen."

Now this made sense. This wasn't about the skylight at all. It was about his wife. Roger had precious memories with his wife in this house.

"Follow me," she said. Sally headed out of the room and stopped when she sensed Roger wasn't following her. "Now!"

If she needed to talk to Roger like he was a five-year-old boy she was going to do it. What he did was wrong on so many levels and she wasn't going to stand for it. Yes, the poor man had some baggage he had to deal with, but she wasn't going to let him act like that. He was sabotaging the sale of his own house.

Stay positive. Everything is going to be fine. Talk with him and send him on his way.

Once in the kitchen she turned around and waited as Roger moved in her direction. He stopped a foot in front of her and avoided eye contact. Good. Maybe he realized what he did was wrong and this would be a one-time episode.

Roger ran a hand through his hair. "I . . ."

"No, Roger. Please don't speak. *You* are in the wrong. I told you not to come here during the open house. You're making my job more difficult. And what's so important that it couldn't wait till later?"

"I told you. I needed to get something out of my office."

"What was it exactly? What did you have to get?"

"A pen."

"A pen . . ." She wondered if Roger took her for a fool. "I do recall seeing a cup of a hundred pens or more at your store. They weren't good enough?"

He pulled the pen from his front jacket pocket. He clicked it a few times. "This one's my favorite." He stuck the pen back in his pocket.

Another car pulled up out front and Sally needed to finish this conversation. "Fine. You've got your pen. Now please go. And don't come back until after four. Got it?"

"Got it."

She walked Roger to the door and opened it. She stepped outside with him as an older couple approached the two of them on the driveway.

"Welcome," said Sally.

"Are you open?" asked the man.

"Absolutely. Please come inside."

"Great. Thank you."

Roger walked to his car with his head down.

Sally did feel sorry for the man but he needed to behave or they'd never sell the house. And if they didn't sell that house, she wouldn't be able to buy *her* house. She had a funny feeling in her gut. Like the odds were stacked against her.

She followed the couple up the path back to the front door.

The woman stopped and pointed to the swing on the magnolia tree. "That thing is a serious liability hazard. No way that would stay."

"I agree," said the man.

Sally swung around to make sure Roger didn't hear that. Wishful thinking.

"I'm sorry?" Roger said, standing in front of the three of them. "Did you say you'd remove the swing if you bought the house?"

Here we go again.

"Yes," said the woman. "The owner of this house is a fool for having it there. He's lucky a neighborhood child hasn't fallen off. The parents would sue him for all he's worth. I'm a lawyer—I've seen these things happen before."

"Well, sorry to tell you that I'm the fool who put that swing there and I'm going to have it stated in the contract that *whoever* buys the house will have to leave it up. And I'll drive by once a week until the day I die to make sure it's still there for the neighborhood kids."

Sally grabbed Roger's arm. "Roger . . ."

Roger peeled Sally's fingers off his arm, patted her hand, and placed it back down by her side. "And if one time I come by and that swing is not where it's supposed to be, I'll sue you for all you're worth. Got it?"

The woman stared at Roger for a few moments. "Then I guess we have no reason to go inside."

"I guess you don't."

"Let's go, honey."

The woman grabbed her husband's hand and left.

Sally glared at Roger. "Roger Hudson . . . prepare to die."

Chapter Eight

The next day Sally was ready for day two of Roger's open house weekend. Once again she had placed her real estate signs on the major cross streets in the neighborhood and opened the front door of his house. It had been a rocky start yesterday and it hadn't gotten any better after that. After Roger had scared away the first two potential buyers at the beginning of the open house, he finally did leave and didn't return. The problem was nobody else visited the open house after that. It was the oddest thing considering the open house she had last weekend attracted almost twenty potential buyers. And this house was much better than that one. There must have been some big festival or sporting event she hadn't heard about that kept people away. She hoped today would be much better. She opened the veggie platter she had picked up from Safeway and pulled a knife out of the drawer to cut open the top of the dip that was giving her a difficult time.

Sally heard the first car and set the knife on the counter.

The first visitor?

She walked to the entryway and peeked out the front door.

"No!"

It was Roger.

She made a beeline for the driveway and threw her arms in the air as he got out of his car. "No. Roger, you're not coming in here."

"I just need to—"

"If you tell me you forgot your favorite pen again I'll scream!"

"It's a pencil this time. A good quality pencil is not easy to come by."

Sally stood there tapping her right foot on the cement.

"Okay, if you want to know, I forgot my lunch."

"Right. You and I both know you'll be eating a tuna sandwich at Highway 9 today."

"You and I both know they're not open on Sundays."

Shoot. He was right.

She needed to get rid of him if she wanted any chance of selling the house. She continued to tap her foot, hoping to think of something else to say.

Roger dropped his gaze to her feet. "That's not good for your shoes. Speaking of which, you're still not wearing the new pair. I don't get it."

"And I don't get why you're here. You expect me to believe you forgot your lunch? If you did, you did it on purpose. Please get a move on."

"Have patience, grasshopper. I'm going inside to get the lunch you don't believe I forgot."

He squeezed her shoulder and walked toward the house.

Sally got zapped from his touch. It was the same feeling she used to get as a child when she stuck her tongue on the end of a battery. She turned and watched him enter the house.

Why did you do that? Knock it off! Don't check out your client's butt!

She waited outside for him. A minute later he returned.

He held up a lunch bag and shook it a few times, rattling the paper. "See?"

The sound of a car horn got both Sally and Roger to turn toward the street.

Maggie waved, got out of her bright pink convertible Smart car and approached the house.

Roger pointed at her car. "You shouldn't leave your toys in the street."

Maggie waved off his comment. "Behave, Roger. Sally, nice to see you."

Sally smiled. "You too, Maggie. You came to see the house?"

"Yes! I've been dying to see the inside for years." Maggie patted Roger on the chest. "But someone has *never* invited me over. Not even once! I've heard about your infamous theater."

Sally's face lit up. "It's amazing!"

Roger raised an eyebrow. "How did you hear about the theater?" He turned and huffed at Sally.

Sally threw her palms up in the air to declare her

innocence. "Not me!"

Maggie squeezed one of his biceps. "No, it wasn't her." She squeezed his bicep a few more times. "Have you been working out, Roger?"

"Answer the question," he said. "Who told you about the theater?"

"Sally, feel his bicep. My goodness!"

Roger grunted. "She's *not* going to feel my bicep."

Maggie winked at Roger. "Her loss."

Sally glanced at his arms. She had the urge to feel them but it wasn't going to happen. Especially given the irritated look on Roger's face. She could see the vein in his forehead getting larger.

"Roger is made of steel," Maggie continued. "Did you know he's single, Sally? He won't give me the time of day but you could—"

Roger brushed her hand off of his arm. "Maggie, tell me who told you about the theater or you're not going inside my house."

"Oh, dear. Okay, let me see. This is a lot of pressure because I really want to go inside. Hmmm." She massaged the bottom of her jaw as she thought about it. "I think it was someone at Safeway." She thought a few moments longer. "Yes! That's it. Sam, the butcher, has a friend whose cousin was a neighbor of the person who used to date the man who sold the materials to the guy who did the art deco ceiling."

Roger grunted.

A black Ferrari rumbled around the corner and zipped right into the driveway like he owned the place. The car stopped inches from Roger's legs. He jumped back and Sally grabbed him to keep him from falling back on his butt. The man had his stereo blasting and his head was bobbing up and down to the beat of the music.

"Who the hell is this jackass?" said Roger.

"He looks familiar," said Maggie. "You know, he's got a striking resemblance to the King of Belgium. I wonder if it's him."

"You honestly think the King of Belgium is driving a Ferrari here in Saratoga?"

"Why not? Anything's possible. You'd better be nice to him, just in case he's royalty."

"I don't care if he's the Fresh Prince of Bel Air—nobody parks in my driveway except me." Roger used his hand to try to shoo the man away like a fly.

The man smirked at Roger and then raised his sunglasses to check out Sally. He winked at her and dropped his glasses back down.

Roger turned to Sally. "Looks like you've got an admirer. Congratulations."

"That's Mark Brannah," said Sally. "He bought the house next door."

Roger stared at the enemy. The man had the balls to park in his driveway. So *this* was the guy who wanted to tear apart the neighborhood and build some ridiculous monstrosity next door. Roger didn't have a single drop of violence in his blood but right now he wanted to punch something. Or some*one*.

Mark got out of his Ferrari and closed the door with his butt. He had a briefcase at his side and a cocky smile on his face.

"What do you want?" asked Roger.

Mark didn't answer. He marched straight inside the house and out of sight.

"Hey!" said Roger. "I'm talking to you!"

Roger ran inside the house after the man and stopped in the family room. "Get out here now."

Where the hell did he go?

Sally and Maggie entered the house.

"Where is he?" asked Maggie.

Roger searched the rooms for Mark but couldn't find the guy. It was like he just disappeared.

Sally pointed to the corner of the backyard. "There he is."

Roger slid open the screen door and walked to the corner of his backyard, where Mark was talking on the phone by the fig tree.

Roger stared him down. "What the hell do you—"

Mark threw up his hand to stop Roger and continued his

conversation on the phone. "Sell the stock when the market opens tomorrow. And get in touch with someone at Apple— they're going to want this app. Gotta go." Mark disconnected and smiled at Roger. "Yes?"

"Don't *yes* me. You're trespassing."

Mark looked around the backyard and chuckled. "You're having an open house. You're telling me you don't allow buyers to see your property at an open house? That's a new one."

"You want to buy my house?"

"I do. You must be Roger Hudson. Great to meet you. I'm Mark Brannah."

Mark extended his hand and Roger stared at it. "I know who you are. You bought the house next door. Why do you want mine?"

Sally joined them in the backyard. "You're interested in the house?"

Mark turned and eyed Sally from head to toe. "Yes." He patted his briefcase. "I brought an offer—fifty percent over the asking price plus a ten percent bonus for the listing agent. Cash deal. We can close in two days. Are you the agent? The file didn't show that Roger remarried."

"You did a background check on me?"

"Of course. Standard procedure if I'm going to do business with anyone."

Sally eyed Roger and then cleared her throat. "I'm Roger's agent. Sally Bright."

Mark stuck out his hand. "Mark Brannah. Pleased to meet you."

Sally shook his hand. "You, too."

Make sure you wash that hand. You don't know where it's been.

Sally gestured toward the house. "Please. Let's go back inside the house."

"Great idea," said Mark.

The guy was dreaming if he thought he was going to buy his house.

Roger followed Sally and Mark back inside his house.

Maggie had her shoes kicked off in the family room and sat with her legs crossed on the loveseat. She flipped through one of Roger's magazines. "This is so much fun! It's almost like camping."

Roger let out a deep breath. "Don't you have somewhere you have to be? Like a *National Enquirer* convention?"

"You're so silly."

Roger grabbed the magazine from Maggie's lap. "This is not a good time, Maggie."

"Oh." She glanced over at Sally and Mark. "Of course, you have business to take care of." She slipped her shoes back on and stood up. "And where's Crouton today?"

"At the store with Jeffrey."

"Wonderful. I'll go pay them both a visit."

"You do that. And buy some shoes while you're there."

After Maggie left Roger turned to Mark. "I'm not interested in your offer."

Mr, Crotchety

Mark opened his briefcase and pulled out some paperwork, handing it to Sally. "Even at the top of the market the best offer in this area with multiple bids ended up selling for twenty percent over the asking price. I'm offering you fifty percent more. You'd be a fool to pass it up."

"Yeah? Well, this fool wants to know why you want my house so bad. I'm pretty sure I know why, but I want to hear it from the horse's mouth."

Mark scratched his chin. "Fair enough. I need space for an Olympic-size swimming pool. Your property is the perfect size."

"Get out."

Mark pointed to the offer. "You don't have to make a decision right now—think about it." He turned to Sally. "Try to talk some sense into him."

Before Sally could answer Mark walked out.

Roger held out his hand. "Let me see that."

Sally handed the offer to Roger. "We can go over it together. Just give me a second while I open this." She grabbed the knife and tried to cut open the top of the vegetable dip container.

"Not necessary—wait here." Roger walked to his office and leaned over the paper shredder, feeding each sheet one by one into the machine.

"No!" yelled Sally from the other room.

A few seconds later she stepped into his office. The knife was still in her hand. She didn't look right. He was so distracted by her red face he almost didn't notice her flaring nostrils. Was she on the verge of hyperventilating? It certainly seemed so. He eyed the knife as it shifted back and forth in her hand. Almost as if she was visualizing how she could slice and dice Roger.

Not good.

The only thing he feared more than a pissed-off woman was a pissed-off woman with a knife.

Make it better. You still need her to sell the house.

"Do you like fish?" he asked.

Sally stared at him like he was crazy. And she wouldn't be far off target with that assumption. The knife dangled between her fingers.

Roger rubbed the back of his neck. "Salmon, more specifically. Do you like salmon?"

The knife stopped moving "Yes. Uh . . . why?"

"Garlic risotto?"

She studied Roger for a moment. "Love it."

"Then it's settled. You'll be my guest for dinner—my way of saying thank you for being my agent. We can talk business too, of course. I'll throw some salmon on the barbecue and make some of my famous garlic risotto. Some garlic bread too. Is that too much garlic in one evening?"

"I . . ."

"Of course not. Glad you agree. Jeffrey and Crouton will be here too."

"Uh . . ."

"Perfect. See you around five."

He slid by her carefully and headed out, wondering what the hell he had just done. Truth be told, he had gotten nervous and hadn't let her speak for fear of her saying no.

Unbelievable.

He'd just invited a woman to join him for dinner. The last time he'd cooked for another woman in his house was over five years ago, for his wife. At least he could use the opportunity this evening to apologize for his behavior.

He had that odd sensation in his body again. As if he'd invited her to dinner because he wanted to spend time with her. Not because he was scared of the knife. And not for business reasons.

What the hell was going on?

Chapter Nine

Five hours later Sally had wrapped up the open house and was at home getting ready before she returned to Roger's for dinner. It turned out to be an amazing afternoon after that paper-shredding ordeal. Sally had confirmation from three different agents that they would submit offers from their clients within the next twenty-four hours. The house would be sold soon. Sally was going to share the news with Roger this evening and couldn't wait. The first phase of her plan was complete. Now on to the second part. She needed to find him a new home ASAP.

She felt some nerves kick in and chewed on one of her nails. What if she couldn't get Roger interested in another place? What if he kept insisting on the Fuscos' house? And worst of all, what if he found out she had lied?

Sally could feel her pulse banging in her head. The temperature seemed to be rising in the room and she was pretty sure she was on the verge of a total freak out.

"Calm down," she whispered to herself.

With her eyes closed, she took in a deep breath and let it out.

She would never forgive herself if she messed this up.

She had to stay focused and on top of her game. Especially since Roger was a distraction. She wouldn't be surprised if some of that anxiety came from the thought of seeing him tonight. But why? She was just meeting with a client, that's all. Yes, a very handsome client with a nice butt. What did that have to do with anything? And why did she happen to be putting on one of the sexiest dresses from her wardrobe? It was just a coincidence. She was in the mood to wear black, that's all. It made perfect sense.

The cell phone rang and Sally reached over, grabbing it off the bed. It was Portia. "I only have a minute. I need to head back over to Roger's. We're having a business dinner and I'm going to share the news with him about the three offers."

"A business dinner?" asked Portia. She had a skeptical tone to her voice.

"Yeah. Why?"

"There's no such thing as a business dinner."

"Of course there is."

"It's after hours. It's social."

"Is not."

"Is, too."

"What are you wearing?"

Sally laughed. "Why does it matter?"

She knew why Portia wanted to know. Her friend was too smart for her own good.

"Tell me," Portia insisted.

She sighed. "My new black dress."

"With the cleavage?"

Sally lifted the neckline of her dress. "There's not *that* much cleavage."

"I knew it!"

"It means nothing at all. I told you—it's business. You've never had dinner with a client before?"

"Never."

"It doesn't matter, I have to get going."

"You sure you want to be Mrs. Crotchety?"

"I'm not going to be Mrs. Crotchety!"

Sally said goodbye and disconnected.

Mrs. Crotchety.

That was the most ridiculous thing she'd ever heard.

Roger pulled the cover off the barbecue and rolled it into place in the middle of the patio. He opened the release on the propane tank and clicked the electric starter. The grill would be ready to go in five or six minutes. And Sally would arrive right around the same time. He whistled as he entered the house to grab the marinated salmon from the refrigerator. Jeffrey was watching over the risotto on the stove top.

Roger pointed to the pot. "Make sure you stir that every couple of minutes until the chicken broth is completely absorbed, but don't smash it."

Jeffrey lifted the top of the pot and stirred the risotto with the spoon. He leaned closer and inhaled. "Man, this smells so good."

"Get your face out of that thing—we don't want your nose hairs in the risotto." Roger pulled the salmon from the refrigerator and continued to whistle as he turned to head back outside.

Jeffrey placed the lid back on the pot and set the spoon down on the counter. "I don't think I've ever heard you whistle before."

Roger stopped and jerked his head back. "I like to whistle."

"You're different today. And you're wearing cologne."

"I always wear cologne."

"Not *that* much."

He stared at his nephew for a moment. He didn't like where this conversation was going and he knew what Jeffrey was thinking. He should send him to go buy some potatoes. In Idaho.

Roger removed the plastic from the top of the marinated salmon and set it aside. "I don't know what you're talking about."

"Uh-huh. I need to get my notepad."

"You stay right there and watch the risotto."

The doorbell rang. Crouton sprang from his bed near the kitchen and sprinted to the front door. "Arf! Arf!"

Roger followed Crouton to the door. "That's right, show her who's boss." He swung the door open and—

Holy cow. Would you look at that!

Sally stood there with a smile on her face—always an impressive sight all by itself. But it was the body-hugging, slim black dress showing off her fantastic frame and legs that was quite possibly going to send him into cardiac arrest.

She bent down to pet Crouton and—

Holy cleavage! Be a gentleman. Look away!

Sally stood back up. "Are you okay?"

"Perfectly fine. Of course. Why do you ask?"

"You're staring at the porch light."

"I thought I saw a spider. Black widow."

Hopefully she didn't think he called *her* a black widow just because she wore black and was dressed to kill.

Sally moved in closer to inspect the porch light and brushed arms with Roger.

Roger jumped back and wiped something imaginary off the doorbell.

Sally leaned in to get a look at his face and he turned away. "What's going on?"

Avoid eye contact. And cleavage contact.

"Nothing," he said. "You hungry?"

"Roger . . ."

"I'm just about ready to put the salmon on."

"Roger, look at me."

Crap.

He turned to look at her and stared at the top of her head. "Yes?"

"Look me in the eyes."

He dropped his gaze a couple of inches lower from her scalp to her eyes. "Okay."

Sally frowned. "What's going on?"

Roger glanced down at her black dress again. "You're . . . breathtaking. A little too much so, if you ask me."

Sally blinked. "Uh . . . okay. Thank you." She studied Roger for a moment. "Now, please tell me what you've done with the real Roger Hudson. You're an impostor."

"What are you talking about?"

"The Roger Hudson *I* know isn't known for handing out compliments."

She was right. What had just happened there? He gave her a compliment, that's what happened. He couldn't remember the last time that had happened. He wanted to take the compliment back. This wasn't good. Being nice to people provoked feelings. He didn't want feelings because feelings gave you yearnings and desires. Next thing you know you get too close to someone and get sucked into some fantasy world of love and bliss and happiness. Then that fateful day comes when the universe pays you a little visit, takes a crap all over your life, and tells you, *Sorry! You can't have that anymore! It's time to suffer!*

Roger wiped his forehead.

Sally leaned in closer. "Are you okay?"

No, I'm not okay. It's that dress. It's making me act like an idiot.

"Roger?"

Jeffrey appeared in the doorway. He smiled and scribbled something in his notebook. "Hi, Sally." He squeezed Roger's shoulder. "I think my wonderful uncle forgot how to entertain, so please come in."

Sally gave Jeffrey a smile. "Thank you. Nice to see you."

She tried to slide by Roger but he moved to the same side and actually blocked her. Then they both shuffled to the other side and did it again.

"Excuse me," she said.

This is embarrassing.

"Sorry," said Roger. "I won't move so you can pass." He stepped back against the door and allowed enough room for Sally to enter. As she passed she looked up and they locked eyes. There was a brief glimpse of something. He wasn't sure what it was. Kindness. Attraction. Connection. Yeah, that's it. He was pretty damn sure they'd had a connection right there. Just for a second or two. Or was it his imagination? Can a woman hypnotize you with her cleavage?

Damn, she smells good, too.

He turned and watched as she followed Jeffrey toward the kitchen in that dress.

Roger looked back out to the street and took a deep breath. He tried to analyze what had just happened.

He had no idea.

Chapter Ten

Sally followed Jeffrey into the kitchen, her mind still on what had just happened on the porch. If she didn't know any better, she would've thought that Roger was nervous. It was cute to see, but it surprised her. Roger "Tough Guy" Hudson was reduced to a complete pile of mush because of a simple piece of material wrapped around her body. She peeked at the reflection of her dress in the glass door of the top oven.

Good choice.

"You smile a lot," said Jeffrey, stirring the risotto. "I like that."

"Thank you. I've got a lot to be grateful for." She leaned in. "That smells wonderful."

"I don't want to take the credit—it's Uncle Roger's recipe. I'm just manning the ship, so to speak."

"And you keep stirring every couple of minutes," said Roger, entering the kitchen. He looked like he had recovered from the incident outside. He pressed the preheat button on the oven and it beeped back at him. Then he pulled a carafe from the refrigerator, holding it up for Sally to see. "Sangria?"

Sally's eyes widened. "Yes! I'd love some."

"His sangria is the best," said Jeffrey. "Homemade. And yes, I'd love some, too."

Roger pulled three glasses from the cupboard and filled them. "I had no doubts about that."

Roger held up his glass. "To . . ."

Sally waited for the toast that never came.

She decided to dive in with a toast of her own. "To the three offers that I'll be receiving on your home."

Roger held his glass in the air and stared at Sally. "Is this wishful thinking or something you know for a fact is going to happen?"

"The latter."

"Alrighty then. Cheers."

They clinked glasses and Sally watched as Roger took a sip of sangria. He set his glass on the counter, picked up the platter of salmon, and headed to the backyard without another word.

Sally turned to Jeffrey. "He didn't seem that happy about the news."

Jeffrey glanced over to Roger in the backyard. "I'm sure it's bittersweet for him. Because of the memories here . . ."

"Yeah."

Jeffrey pointed the spoon at his uncle. "He's a good guy."

Sally nodded. "I've seen glimpses."

Jeffrey laughed. "You're a good influence on him, so thank you. It hasn't been easy to watch him over the last five years. I love him so much but he's been a broken man. Since

I'm studying human behavior at San Diego State, it's fascinating and sad at the same time."

"Losing someone isn't easy. People give you advice on how to deal with it, but I think every person is different and it's not a one-size-fits-all plan."

"True. You seem to know a lot about it. Have you lost someone?"

She stared at Jeffrey for a moment. "Let's just say . . . I almost lost myself."

Jeffrey squished his eyebrows together. "I don't understand. You mean you almost died?"

She nodded. "And that seems to change your perspective on things. It opens your eyes and shows you how fragile life is. So I don't take it for granted anymore." Sally couldn't believe she'd told this to Roger's nephew but maybe he'd learn something from her experience.

"Can I ask you what happened? I mean, if you don't mind talking about it."

Sally smiled and looked outside to see if Roger was paying attention. He was in the corner of the yard fidgeting with the bird feeder. "Of course. It was breast cancer."

"No wonder you're always so happy." He seemed to be thinking about it. "My Aunt Macy wasn't so lucky."

"Millions of women aren't so lucky. Like I said before, I'm filled with gratitude."

"You beat it. Good for you. And I for one am glad you kicked cancer's butt. I'm very happy to have met you.

Hopefully my uncle will learn from you. He's a bit stubborn, though. Sometimes I think he says things just to get a reaction out of people."

Sally laughed. "You know what they call him around town?"

"Mr. Crotchety?"

"You know!"

"Even *he* knows. He's been called much worse—I've heard it with my own ears. Some woman called him a useless bag of horse dung."

"I didn't know horse dung came in bags. Paper or plastic?"

Jeffrey and Sally shared a laugh together and Roger came back in. He placed the empty platter in the sink and put some water in it. He turned around and looked at Sally. Then Jeffrey. "What's so funny?"

Jeffrey laughed even harder. "Nothing at all."

Roger grunted.

He opened the pantry door and flipped open the top of the container of dog food on the floor. He grabbed the cup and scooped some dog food out. "Crouton! Soup's on!"

Crouton came screeching from around the corner and slid into Roger's feet. "Arf! Arf!"

Roger held the cup in Sally's direction. "You wanna feed him?"

Crouton's eyes followed the cup in the air. "Arf!"

"Oh." Sally sat her glass of sangria on the island

counter. "I'd love to." She took the cup of food from Roger and looked around for Crouton's food bowl. "Where?"

Roger walked around to the other side of the island and pointed to the bowl on the floor. "Right there. Pour it in the bowl quickly and stand back. The dog is a savage and may bite your arm off."

Sally laughed. "Okay." She poured the food into the bowl and stood back. He was right—Crouton attacked the food like it was his last meal on earth. He grunted as he ate; it was the cutest thing.

"Chew your food," said Roger. "You've got a couple of straight teeth—use 'em."

Sally laughed again and watched Roger's body language. He pretended he didn't like the dog but she could see quite clearly the man adored Crouton. Roger had a container of dog treats on the kitchen counter. Same as the treats she saw in a plastic bag at the shoe store. Crouton had a dog bed in every single room in the house, including the theater. Plus, there were dog toys scattered all over the place. No way a person who didn't like dogs would buy those things. Roger wasn't fooling anybody.

Crouton finished his food and looked up with his funny face and dark brown eyes.

"This is the part I don't like." Roger reached down and grabbed Crouton and held him away from his body, moving outside at a brisk pace. He set Crouton on the back lawn and took a few steps back. Curious, Sally grabbed Roger's sangria and brought it outside for him.

Roger threw his hand in the air. "Don't come any closer, he's about to let one go. It's like clockwork after a meal. The dog has more gas than Chevron."

Sally smiled and handed Roger his sangria. "You tried to fool me before and now you're doing it again."

Roger cocked his head to the side. "What are you talking about?"

She held out her sangria and toasted him. "You're an old softy. I told you. You have a crusty exterior but deep down you're as sweet as blueberry pie."

"Last time you said apple pie. Which one is it?"

"I changed my mind." Sally clinked his glass again. "Blueberry pie is sweeter."

Roger grunted and opened the barbecue, looking inside. "Almost forgot about this." He flipped the salmon so the skin was on top. "Just going to seal in the juices and give it some grill marks on top."

Roger was good at changing the subject. He'd had practice, obviously. Once again he wasn't fooling her. She decided to cut him some slack and let the subject go.

A few seconds later Sally heard something odd and scanned the yard in search of the sound. It was like someone was letting air out of a balloon.

Roger pointed to Crouton. "I warned you."

"Oh, God." Sally fanned the air in front of her face. "I think I'll go inside."

"Great. Leave me here for dead."

Sally laughed.

"Tell Jeffrey to stick the garlic bread in the oven. Then transfer the risotto into the green serving dish on the table. We're going to eat in exactly three minutes."

"Sounds great."

Roger let out a deep breath and watched Sally as she walked back into the house. Seriously, that dress had to be illegal in certain states. And if not, it should be a crime for any woman to look that sexy, that gorgeous, that irresistible.

Damn.

It was also hard to believe there was an actual woman in his house. Yes, she had been there before, but that had been for business. She was his agent, but this didn't feel exactly like business. It felt like he was cooking for a woman who had come to visit. A very attractive woman.

Giving the salmon one more minute before he pulled it from the grill, he glanced inside the house again at Sally. Jeffrey had stuck the garlic bread in the oven and was now holding the pot while Sally used the wooden spoon to scrape the risotto into the green serving bowl. Roger continued to watch her. She was an amazing woman. Full of life. Full of love.

He had gotten her all wrong.

He ventured to guess that the only reason she annoyed him so much in the beginning was because he was jealous of her happiness. He wanted to be just as happy as her. Yes, he had had that level of happiness back when he was married, but that was long ago and he missed it. He couldn't help but feel that the beautiful real estate agent inside of his home was changing him back to the way he used to be. No, he wasn't a completely changed man. Not even close. But it felt like he was moving in the right direction. He'd been stuck in a funk for years and it felt like there was finally light at the end of the tunnel. Either that or he was drunk from the sangria.

"Geez, Louise!" Roger was so deep in his thoughts he had forgotten about the salmon. He lifted the lid of the barbecue and pulled the salmon from the grill.

He joined Sally and Jeffrey inside, setting the platter on the table. "You two start serving yourselves." Roger pulled the garlic bread from the oven and used the tongs to place the pieces in a basket. He covered the bread with a cloth and placed it on the center of the table.

Roger sat and raised his glass again. This time he wasn't tongue-tied. "To food."

Sally toasted him. "To the chef!"

"Yes!" said Jeffrey. "To the chef."

They toasted and Roger took a sip of his sangria.

Now's the time. Apologize. Do it.

Roger cleared his throat and held out his glass again. "To women who find it in their hearts to forgive bitter men who act like complete jackasses at open houses or anywhere else in the world at any given time."

Sally smiled. "Cheers."

"Amen!" said Jeffrey, taking a large gulp of his sangria.

Roger gave him a look. "Eat your food."

"I don't have a problem with that." Jeffrey winked at his uncle and then took a bite of the salmon. He moaned and took a bite of the risotto. Another moan. Then a bite of the garlic bread. "Can I toast the chef again?"

"No. And you sound like Crouton when you eat. Try chewing your food."

Roger felt better after the toast. During the dinner the three of them talked about Jeffrey's studies, shoes, and food.

Sally took another sip of her sangria and smiled. "We can start looking for your new home soon."

Roger wiped his mouth and placed the napkin back on his lap. "Great. I don't want any lag time in between the sale of my home and the purchase of the new one. The last thing I want is to have to rent a place or stay in a hotel if I don't find a new home in time."

"Understood. I'll be able to show you some homes as early as tomorrow afternoon if that works for you. I just need to get your preferences and do a little research to see what's available."

"Don't forget the Fuscos' home as part of your research."

"I won't."

Jeffrey stood and grabbed his plate. "I think that's my cue since you're going to talk business. Can I watch a movie in the theater?"

"Of course."

Sally sat up and placed the fork on her plate. "What types of movies do you like?"

Jeffrey rinsed his plate and stuck it in the dishwasher. "The classics. Just like Uncle Roger."

"I didn't think that was common for someone your age and gender."

Jeffrey laughed and placed a few more things in the dishwasher. "It's not. I guess my old uncle rubbed off on me."

Roger stood up and grabbed both his and Sally's plates from the table and set them on the counter. "Who you calling old? You have a death wish?"

Jeffrey picked up his notebook and pretended to write in it. "Threatened with violence by uncle. Not good. Subject needs help and quite possibly some Valium."

Sally laughed and helped clear a few more things from the table. "Are you really studying Roger?"

Jeffrey closed the notebook and dropped it on the kitchen island. "His every move. Mostly how he interacts with people. Or how he doesn't interact with them."

Roger grabbed the kitchen towel that hung from the handle on the stove and snapped it at Jeffrey's butt. A direct hit.

Jeffrey screamed and rubbed his butt. "Hey!" He reached for his notebook. "Child abuse."

"You're in your twenties. And don't even think about writing that down. Don't you have a movie to watch?"

"Yeah. You have *An Affair to Remember*, right?"

"Of course."

Sally lit up. "I *love* that movie. Haven't seen it in ages."

"Well . . ." said Jeffrey. He glanced at Roger and then back at Sally. "I can wait until after you're done with your business and we can watch it together."

"Oh . . ." Sally glanced over at Roger, fidgeting a little. It was as if she wanted to watch the movie but thought it would be inappropriate. Maybe she had looked to Roger for his approval.

Say something, you fool.

Roger raised his palms. "Don't look at me. If you want to watch the movie with Jeffrey I'm not going to stop you."

I might be a little jealous, though.

Jeffrey wiped his hands on the kitchen towel. "You can watch it too, obviously. After all, it's your house and your theater."

Now it was Roger's turn to look to Sally for approval. Why? He had no idea. He didn't need approval from anyone. Still. It felt as if Jeffrey and Sally had agreed to watch the movie together and he was the lone man out. Crouton didn't count.

"Roger?" said Sally.

Uh-oh. He was pretty sure she had said something and he'd missed it.

"Yes?"

Sally smiled and rubbed the side of Roger's arm. "I said you have to watch it with us."

Roger stared at her hand on his arm and she quickly pulled it away. "Fine. But I always make popcorn with fresh butter. Is that a problem?"

"I never turn down anything with butter."

"And I have to have chocolate-covered raisins with every movie."

"I never turn down anything with chocolate, either."

"And Red Vines."

"Two of my favorite words . . ."

"Then we're in agreement. Good."

He finished cleaning the kitchen and put things away, then headed to the theater where Jeffrey and Sally were seated. Crouton trailed along and went directly to his bed.

Roger started the popcorn maker and handed Sally a box of Red Vines and chocolate-covered raisins.

Her eyes widened. "Yummy. Thank you."

She placed the boxes of candy on her lap. The lap comprised of a sexy black dress. A sexy black dress that had happened to slide up her legs a little.

Man, oh, man.

This didn't make sense at all. Roger had built up an immunity to women over the last five years. He had trained his mind to believe they did absolutely nothing for him. There had been more than a fair share of women who had come to the shoe store after they found out he was a widower. Looking for a man to take care of. Looking for a man who was vulnerable. Looking for a sugar daddy. Some had brought casseroles. Some had brought books on healing. Others were more blunt and had asked him out on a date. But he was proud of how swiftly and easily he had been able to dismiss them all. They could have walked in his store naked and it wouldn't have made a difference.

But this Sally creature . . . Yeah, she was a creature, all right.

Nothing else could explain the effect she had on him. Those damn legs and the rest of her were going to kill him. He felt things he hadn't felt since back when he had met Macy the first time. He wanted to pursue Sally to the end of the earth, but he also wanted to shut the idea down immediately.

Uh-oh.

He just realized he had been standing right in front of Sally checking out her legs for the last few seconds. Hopefully she would think he was eyeing the candy on her lap.

She lifted the box of chocolate-covered raisins. "Should we open them now? It looks like you want some."

He decided the best course of action was to keep his mouth shut. He forced a smile and nodded.

"Okay . . ." Sally opened the box and held it over

Roger's open palm. She jiggled the box so some of the chocolate covered raisins slid out onto his hand.

"Thanks." He popped them all in his mouth at once. "The popcorn will be ready in a moment and then we'll get started."

"Great!" Sally held out the box toward Jeffrey.

Jeffrey shook his head. "I'm good, thanks. By the way, I've seen this movie three times. This will be number four."

"I've seen it at least five times."

"Ha!" said Roger, handing Sally and Jeffrey bags of fresh-popped popcorn. "I've seen it thirty-five times."

Sally raised an eyebrow. "Right."

"Actually," said Jeffrey, "he's telling the truth."

"Really?"

Roger served one more bag of popcorn for himself and sat next to Sally. "It's not that difficult. Once a year over the last thirty-five years."

Sally grabbed a few fingers of popcorn from her bag. "Yeah, I guess when you break it down like that once a year doesn't seem crazy. What is it about this movie? Why is it so popular? I mean, I know it's romantic. But it's got something else that makes it special. A classic."

Roger thought about it for a moment. "The movie is about what everybody wants. Unconditional love. Loving no matter what. Call it finding your soulmate or destiny or whatever, but they had to be on that cruise ship at the same time. They had to meet and end up together. Didn't matter their circumstances or if one of them suffered a tragedy. It was meant to be. *That's* why the movie is so popular."

Sally didn't respond.

Did he sound like a blabbing idiot? Next time he'd know better than to speak from the heart. Better to keep his mouth shut. He glanced over again to see the expression on her face.

Sally shifted in her chair to look Roger in the eyes. "Roger Hudson, you're such a romantic."

Roger grunted and played it off. "It was just something I read in a magazine. *Cosmo*, maybe."

Sally stared at him.

"Uh . . . there could have been a *Cosmo* at the dentist. Yeah. And it was the only thing there to read."

Sally opened the box of Red Vines. "Right."

Jeffrey stood and winked at Roger. "Go ahead and start the movie without me. I just thought of something important for my thesis and need to get it out of my brain before I forget it."

Roger opened the arm of the chair and pulled out the remote. "We can wait if it's only going to take a few minutes."

"No, that's okay. I think I'll need more time than that. Start it and I'll sneak back in when I'm done."

Roger pressed a few buttons on the remote. The movie screen lit up in front of them and the lights dimmed in the theater. Then he pressed *menu* and selected the movie.

A few seconds later the movie began. And a few seconds after that, Crouton snored like a hippo.

Roger leaned over the end of the chair and looked down to the floor. "Stick a sock in it."

Sally laughed. "Crouton is so cute."

"You want him?"

Sally playfully slapped Roger on the arm. "You know you'd never give up Crouton. He's your little buddy."

"I'll pay you to take him. How about a thousand bucks? Five thousand?"

"Nice try. I can read you like a—"

"Shhhh! It's starting. I love this song and the snow falling in Central Park."

Roger had to admit it was great to have Sally's company. If he had to count he'd say he only glanced over at her or checked out her legs fifty times during the movie.

The end of the movie came and Roger did his best to maintain control. That last scene was very emotional and there was no way in hell he was going to cry in front of Sally.

Suck it up.

Fortunately, he was able to hold it together without looking like a wimp. As Cary Grant pulled in Deborah Kerr for an embrace and a kiss at the end, Roger glanced over to Sally.

Unbelievable. She had fallen asleep during the climax of the movie.

At least she didn't snore like Crouton.

She looked so peaceful as she slept. Like an angel. What a beautiful woman. Hell, she was a knockout and he now couldn't take his eyes off of her. And out of nowhere feelings crept into his system. Urges. He couldn't comprehend what was on his mind.

He wanted to kiss her on the forehead. And he wanted to do it so badly. Jeffrey wasn't around so there was no chance of being seen or being documented. Should he do it? He was pretty sure he was going to.

This could be a huge mistake. Please don't wake up.

He was going in.

Roger leaned down careful not to wake her and kissed Sally on the forehead. He held his lips there for a few seconds and then pulled away. Her skin was smooth and her hair smelled wonderful. Like strawberries.

The music continued to play and the credits rolled. He sat back in his seat and wondered when she would wake up. It didn't matter.

There was now silence in the room.

He closed his eyes for a moment and enjoyed it.

A few seconds later Crouton snorted in his sleep and Sally jumped. She yawned and stared at the blank screen for a few moments, then turned to look at Roger. "Oh . . ."

Roger chuckled. "Yeah. Oh. You fell asleep."

What was going on inside of that pretty head of hers? She locked eyes with him and then her gaze dropped to his lips. Roger's heart rate sped up. Sally was looking at his lips.

Oh, boy.

Now he contemplated kissing her again. This time on the lips.

Should I do it? Is that what she wants? I want to be a mind reader!

Then, just like that, the moment was gone.

Sally pushed away and adjusted her dress. "Sorry about that. I can't believe I fell asleep. Was I out long?"

"Just a couple of minutes, I think."

She stood and reached for the empty box of chocolate-covered raisins and Red Vines.

Roger stood and ran his hand through his hair. "Leave that—I'll get it later. I can drive you home since you're sleepy."

"No, no." She avoided eye contact with him. "I'll be okay. Thanks again for the wonderful dinner and movie. I'll give you a call tomorrow. Plan on looking at houses in the afternoon."

"Sounds good."

Roger didn't like her body language. Something was wrong. Crap. Did she know he had kissed her on the forehead? What a foolish thing to do. She was his real estate agent!

Sally avoided eye contact and headed to the kitchen. She grabbed her purse that hung from the chair and moved toward the door. No words. No beautiful smiles. Nothing.

Roger jumped in front of her and opened the front door for her.

"Thanks again," she said.
Then she was gone.

Chapter Eleven

"Hang on!" said Sally, talking with Portia the next morning. She tossed the phone on the bed and slipped on her white skirt. Then she pulled a lilac blouse over her head and checked herself out in the mirror.

Perfect.

Comfortable. Professional. No cleavage.

She loved the way Roger had looked at her last night, like she was the most beautiful woman in the world, but she needed to get serious and find him a house today.

She grabbed the phone from the bed. "Roger kissed me on the forehead last night!"

"Yes!"

"But he doesn't even know *I know* he kissed me."

"Wait. How is that possible he doesn't know you know he kissed you? Hold on, I'm getting some sort of a déjà vu. Yeah, this reminds me of a movie. Which one was it? Oh, oh, oh . . . that one with Rachel McAdams where she meets that guy in some weird club where it's pitch dark. They chat for a long time without knowing what the other person looks like and they have a wonderful chat! Then they leave the club and go outside and find out what the other person looks like.

And they were both pleasantly surprised! What was that movie?"

"*About Time.*"

"Yes! Love that movie. So, is that what happened?"

"No! I haven't been to a club since Bon Jovi was living on a prayer. Roger kissed me and I pretended I was asleep."

"You were in bed?"

"Things are so difficult to explain to you sometimes. Okay, don't speak and I'll explain. We were watching *An Affair to Remember.*"

"Love that movie."

"I know, but don't speak."

"Sorry."

"Anyway, it was the end of the movie and the part I was waiting for."

"Deborah Kerr is on the couch and Cary Grant pulls her in for a wonderful embrace."

"I'm going to hang up on you."

"My mouth is zipped now."

"So, I like to sometimes close my eyes during that part and pretend I'm there and Cary Grant is kissing me. But my fantasy of *Cary* turned into the reality of *Roger* when I felt his lips on my forehead. It was *so* hard to pretend I was asleep. I almost jumped out of my skin. We were inches apart. I could hear him breathing and could feel his heat. I could smell that wonderful fresh scent of his—a mix of citrus and buttered popcorn. And I was feeling warm feelings!"

Portia screamed. "I love warm feelings!"

"Me, too!"

"Speaking of which, I met someone."

Sally stared at the phone. She must have heard her wrong. After Portia's messy divorce she had gone on a mission to eliminate everything in her life that was connected to a penis. Any DVD or romance novel with a man on the cover was donated to Goodwill. Male singers in her iTunes were deleted. She unfriended every man on Facebook. She changed cubicles at the office and moved to the corner where she was positioned in between a female agent and the wall. She cut her hair super-short thinking it would scare the men away. Instead, her bold new look made her appear more confident and attracted even more men than before. Sally laughed at the thought of her having met someone despite the precautions she'd taken.

"Did you just say you had met someone?"

"Yes."

"What happened to the woman I knew who said no more men?"

Portia laughed. "That woman is *gone*. The harder I tried to avoid men the more they kept showing up."

"Okay, enough with the suspense. Just tell me who he is and how you met."

"First, his name is Jeffrey."

"That's such a nice name. In fact, it's the name of Roger's—"

"Nephew."

No. Portia wouldn't dare. Sally listened through the phone and she didn't hear anything. Not a good sign.

"Portia?"

Portia giggled. Also not a good sign. "Yes?"

"Please tell me you don't have the hots for Roger's nephew."

"Do you want me to tell you the truth or tell you what you want to hear?"

"No!" Sally paced back and forth in her living room and tried to wrap her head around what she just had found out. Portia and Jeffrey. Jeffrey and Portia. There was no way it could work out. She was like twice his age!

"Portia?"

Another giggle. "Yes?"

"You're forty years old."

"Thanks for reminding me."

"And he's like, what? Twenty-four?"

"You got it."

"Oh, wow. Roger is going to kill you. How did this happen?"

"I went to try that world famous ham and Swiss you raved about at Highway 9. As I ate outside at one of the tables I saw a man cross the street from Roger's store. The closer he got, the better looking he got. That man is gorgeous! Anyway, he sat next to me, we talked and I ended up asking him out."

"*You* asked *him* out?"

"I know! Crazy. Anyway, we're going out tonight."

This was insane. How could it end with a happy ending? Portia was sixteen years older than Jeffrey. Plus he had to go back south and finish his degree. Did Portia know that?

"You know he's going back to San Diego at the end of summer, right?"

"Of course, he has to finish his graduate thesis. That man is smart. And let me tell you something, he knows exactly what a woman wants."

"You figured this out over a ham and Swiss?"

"Oh, yeah. I can't wait for our date tonight. And it sounds like your date last night was a success if he kissed you?"

"It wasn't a date! And we didn't kiss. Foreheads don't count."

Although last night at Roger's felt like a date.

Portia laughed. "Call it whatever you want to call it. It still comes up as a date. Glad to hear it after what you've been through, sweetie."

Sally's divorce had been painful, but she had never given up on love. She had just decided to stay focused on her career and hopefully the right man would come along when it was time. Her thoughts went to Roger and she felt a little giddy.

"Are you there?" asked Portia.

"Yeah. Just thinking of Roger."

"Not a surprise."

Sally sat at the desk in her home office. "I can't believe I forgot to tell you he's interested in the Fuscos' home."

"No! What did he say when you told him you wanted to buy it?"

Sally didn't answer.

"Sally? You did tell him, right?"

"No."

"Why not?"

"Because I can't make an offer on a house and then represent someone who makes an offer on the same house. You know it's a conflict of interest. That would mean I'd have to give him up as a client which means I wouldn't have the commission to buy that house. It's a lot easier just to find him another house."

"Did you ever think that if you told him you wanted to buy the house yourself he may let you buy it?"

Nope. She hadn't thought of that.

Sally let out a deep breath. "Or he may still want it."

"I've never seen you tell a lie in your life! It's not you."

Portia was right. Sure, Sally had told little white lies to protect people's feelings. Lies like "Your new dress is beautiful" and "This tastes so good!" but lies like that never hurt those people, did they?

"I think you're making a mistake," added Portia.

"Maybe you're right. But I'm going to find him an amazing house he'll love and everybody will be happy."

At least that's what she hoped.

"It's impossible for that window to get any cleaner." Jeffrey moved closer to his uncle in the display in front of the store. "Seriously. I think you're starting to remove the glass."

Roger stopped wiping and stood up straight. "Very funny." Jeffrey stared at him like he had a mushroom growing out of his head. "Don't look at me that way."

"What way is that, my dear uncle?"

"And don't you *dear uncle* me, either. It's that same look you give me right before you write something foolish in that damn journal of yours. I'm telling you I'll send you home. And I'll shred everything you've written about me, too."

"You'd never do anything like that to your sweet nephew, so nice try. What's been on your mind? I can see something is going on."

He certainly wasn't going to tell his nephew about what had happened last night with Sally. That would have been just another golden nugget that ended up in his thesis. He didn't answer and took a swig of his water.

Jeffrey smirked. "This must have something to do with the kiss last night."

Roger wished his nephew would've waited until after he'd swallowed the water before he'd dropped that bomb on him. The water shot out of his mouth and sprayed Jeffrey in the face.

Jeffrey wiped his cheeks and nose with his hand. "I take it you're surprised that I know?" His eyes grew wider. "Uh-oh." Jeffrey pointed to the front display window. The glass looked like it was covered with hundreds of tiny rain droplets.

Roger took a deep breath. "I'm feeling kind of twitchy all of a sudden."

"Let me get that." Jeffrey grabbed the towel to dry the glass.

Roger nearly fell over. How the hell did his nephew know about the kiss? "Explain."

Jeffrey sprayed the glass with window cleaner and started the cleaning process all over again. "Okay. I was going to the kitchen for some water and heard the end of the movie. What can I say? I love that part! So I peeked in and saw your lips on Sally's forehead."

"Unbelievable."

"What's the big deal? If I were in your place I would've kissed her, too."

Roger jerked his head back. "And I would've killed you."

Jeffrey grabbed his notebook and opened it.

This madness never ends.

His nephew clicked his pen a few times and wrote in his notebook. "Signs of jealousy. Another death threat. Not good."

Roger grabbed the bottle and towel from Jeffrey and

touched up the window. "I might as well tell you. Last night was the first night in five years that I didn't think of your Aunt Macy before I went to sleep. My thoughts were on Sally. And I feel horrible about it."

"Aunt Macy would want you to move on."

Roger grunted. "I *have* moved on. But that doesn't mean I stop thinking about her or stop missing her. Anyway, let's drop the subject. Sally will be here soon to pick me up. We're going to go look at a few houses. I have no idea what time I'll be home so after you lock up here, you may want to grab yourself a bite to eat on the way home." Roger stopped wiping for a moment and took another sip of his water.

"Not necessary," said Jeffrey. "I have a date."

Water sprayed Jeffrey in the face again.

"Damn!" Roger wiped his mouth and sat in the chair. "Quit telling me things like that when I have a mouth full! And how could you have a date? And *why* would you date? You're going back to San Diego."

Jeffrey wiped his face again. "What does that have to do with anything? I met an amazing woman and she asked me out."

"She asked *you* out?"

"Hey, you've had women come in here and ask you out, so don't look so surprised."

True. Jeffrey was a good-looking and intelligent man. Still, why would he waste time going out with someone if he knew it wasn't going to go anywhere?

"Besides," Jeffrey continued. "We could become good friends. You never know."

"Did you accept the dinner date thinking you could possibly become friends?"

Jeffrey grinned. "No way. She's a beautiful woman and I'm very attracted to her. And I love that she's older."

Roger studied his nephew for a moment. "How much older are we talking here?"

"Well, I didn't come right out and ask her—I'm not a fool. But I'm going to assume she's in her mid to late thirties."

"You're going out with a cougar! I'll kill her. How dare she take advantage of my—"

"She's not a cougar."

"Right. Does she want to have sex with you?"

"Hopefully."

Roger ground his teeth. "Jeffrey . . ."

"I'm kidding! Look, it's just dinner, that's all. She's smart and fun and I like that. And age doesn't matter anyway. How old is Sally?"

"What does that have to do with anything? We're not going out."

"I didn't say you were. But she's about ten years younger than you, right?"

"Maybe."

"And you wouldn't go out with her because of that?"

"That's different."

"Do you find Sally attractive?"

That would be a *hell, yes,* but Roger wasn't going to say anything. This nephew of his was really starting to annoy him. Why wouldn't he let up on the Sally situation? It was as if he were trying to force them together. Is that why Brenda sent Jeffrey to stay with him? To help him find a woman?

Roger pointed to Jeffrey's chest with his index finger. "I'm on to you. You didn't have to work on your thesis last night. You set it up so Sally and I would be alone. Admit it."

"Okay, I admit it. And you need to admit you like her and find her attractive."

Roger grunted.

Crouton got up from his bed, matched Roger's grunt, and moved toward the front door. "Arf! Arf!"

Jeffrey put his hand on Roger's shoulder and stopped him from turning around. "Quit thinking so much and just answer the question. Do you think Sally's an attractive woman?"

"She's one of the most beautiful women I have ever laid eyes on! But that has nothing to do with anything at all. She's my agent and that's where it ends."

Jeffrey grinned and looked over Roger's shoulder. "Oh . . . hi Sally! I didn't hear you come in."

Roger swung around. Sure enough, Sally was standing right there. And there were those sexy legs again. Inside his store. Crouton was on his back, enjoying a belly rub from Roger's "agent."

Damn.

His chest tightened and he adjusted his collar. "Sally . . ."

"Roger . . ."

He cleared his throat. "How much of our conversation did you hear?"

"Enough."

Roger adjusted his collar again. "Okay, this is awkward. Look, here's what we're going to do. We're going to put this behind us and focus on why you're here. You're my real estate agent, yes or no?"

"Yes."

"And *you* are going to help me find me a house to live in. Yes or no?"

"Yes."

"That's it."

"That's it."

Roger ran his hand through his hair. "Good. Glad we got this cleared up. Let's go."

Chapter Twelve

Roger was mortified. He sat in the passenger seat of Sally's car as she drove them to see the first house on her list. He had put his foot in his mouth again but this time *really* well. Sally now knew he thought she was attractive. And who knew if she had any idea he had kissed her last night. One thing was certain, his nephew couldn't be trusted anymore.

He glanced over to Sally, who was focused on driving. He tried to keep his focus off her legs. She hadn't spoken a word in the car since they had left his store. Who could blame her? She was just doing what she was told. They had a business relationship and he made sure she knew it. But now he was second-guessing himself and he didn't know what to do. Had he sounded mean when he said it? He didn't think so. And since when did he care if he sounded mean?

One thing still bothered him. Her legs. He had no willpower and had to take a peek. Just a little peek. He shot his eyes toward her legs and then got them back on the road. That was great. He was able to look without turning his head so there was no way she could have known he was—

"I saw that," she said.

"Sorry."

"Is that professional? Looking at your real estate agent's legs?"

Very well played. And she was right.

"It won't happen again," he said with zero confidence. "Tell me about the houses we're going to see. Is the Fuscos' place one of them?"

"No. The house isn't ready. For now we've got others to look at."

"Okay, tell me about the first house for today then."

"Of course. It has everything you want. Privacy. Nature. Island in the kitchen. Large master bedroom. Two car garage. Walk-in shower. Large spare room for the theater. Completely remodeled and ready to move in."

"Good."

Sally pulled into the entrance of a private community and inched up to the security gate. She typed a code into a keypad and the gate slid open. She drove through and pulled in one of the visitor parking spots near the clubhouse.

Roger eyed the property. There were mature trees everywhere. He lowered his window. It was quiet except for someone swimming in the pool.

"I had no idea this place was here."

"It's an over-fifty-five community." Sally opened her door. "Okay, let's go see."

"Wait a minute."

Sally pulled her sexy leg back in the car. "Everything okay?"

"No. Everything's not okay. Does this place have homeowner association fees?"

"Yes, but it's—"

"Next."

"But—"

"Next!"

Sally sat there for a moment, staring at Roger. "Listen, Mr. Crotchety . . ."

Roger's mouth fell open. "Did you really just call your client that?"

"Yes. Got a problem with it?"

"Not at all. It just caught me off guard coming from you. It's not like I haven't heard it before."

Sally laughed and the sweet sound made Roger smile. What he didn't expect was for the laughter to grow. Fuller, deeper, louder. The ice was broken and Roger joined her in the laugh. In fact, he got cramps from laughing and Sally had to wipe tears from her eyes.

A minute later the laughter was gone. The two of them sat there out of breath looking at each other and wondering what the heck just happened. It was like one of those tropical rain storms in Hawaii that swept in for two or three minutes and soaked everything. Then, out of nowhere, the sun shined and brought with it the most amazing rainbow.

Sally lowered her window and took in a deep breath of air. Roger decided to do the same. He felt peace. He couldn't remember the last time he had laughed like that. It felt amazing—like an injection of vitamins or caffeine.

He inhaled again and let it out. "How much are the HOA fees here?"

"One hundred and fifty a month. Very reasonable considering it covers the roof, water, garbage, and the pool."

"You're right—very reasonable. Okay, let's go see the home."

He swung his door open and waited for Sally to get out of the car. She looked at him like he was crazy and she was probably right. Something had happened in the car when they shared that laugh together. He wasn't sure what it was but it felt like he'd had a giant weight taken off his shoulders.

They walked side by side toward the end of the street and made a right in the direction of the home with the "For Sale" sign. She got the key from the lockbox out front and they entered the property.

They went through every room and it was a beautiful home.

Roger opened the door to the garage and paused. "Oh."

"What?"

"A one-car garage."

Sally blinked. "I don't know how that happened. The system said it had two garages. I'm so sorry."

"It's okay. Let's move on. What's next?"

"Okay. A four bedroom-three bath over by the high school."

He grimaced. "How close to the high school?"

"Five streets away, but it's on a court."

"As much as I love the kids that doesn't sound peaceful to me. I'd be able to hear the football games on Friday nights."

"You're right. Then let's move on to the third one. It's up in the hills above Saratoga. Totally secluded."

"I love it already."

They hopped back in the car and Sally drove up Pierce Road about a mile. She pulled up to a driveway with a chain across the entrance. She got out and pulled the key from the lockbox and unlocked the chain, moving it out of the way. The driveway zig-zagged around a few trees and they came into a clearing where the house stood. It was one of those log cabin type houses you would typically see in Lake Tahoe or Bear Valley. All Roger could hear when they got out of the car was a few birds and squirrels. No sound of people, cars, or streets. Secluded, just like Sally had said.

He loved it.

After they toured the house they went into the backyard and looked around. There was a small patio surrounded by an oval-shaped lawn. A few lounge chairs and tables decorated the backyard as well as some tiki torches. Huge boulders and cactus lined the perimeter of the yard and on the driveway side there was a drop of almost thirty feet that went down to the canyon below. Completely in nature and exactly what Roger wanted.

He pointed to a path in between two of the boulders. "Is that a hiking trail?"

"I don't know. Let's see."

Roger followed Sally as she walked around one of the largest boulders and headed down a slight incline. A couple of steps on the dirt and her foot slid out from under her, causing her to bang into one of the boulders. Roger lunged forward to try to grab her before she hit the ground but it was too late.

"Are you okay?" he asked.

She had hit that boulder pretty hard.

Sally stood up with the help of Roger and brushed off some of the dirt that stuck to her white skirt. "I'm fine. I'm sure I'll have a nasty bruise there but I'm a tough girl." She tried to brush her skirt clean a little more and winced. "Ouch." She hiked up her skirt just a couple of inches and revealed a scrape the size of a tennis ball.

Roger pointed to it. "That's a nasty scrape. Let's head back to the yard. I can clean you up."

"I'll be okay." She touched it and winced again.

Roger held out his hand. "Come on."

Sally stared at his hand for a moment and then took it. Roger led her back to the yard and toward the lawn chair. "Sit there and don't move."

Sally did as she was told while Roger turned on the water against the back of the house. He pulled the hose toward her and placed it on the lawn momentarily.

She pointed to the hose. "You gonna give me a bath?"

Now why did she have to ask that? He needed to stay

focused on cleaning up her wound and the last thing he needed was to picture her naked. "Okay, let your injured leg hang over the edge of the chair and I'm going to clean it up as much as I can. Let's see it."

Sally stared up at him. "Uh . . ."

"Come on, we're two adults here. I promise not to gawk . . . too much."

Sally slid her skirt up to reveal the wound.

Roger wiped his forehead. "Geez, Louise."

"That bad?"

"No. It's just going to be a lot harder to concentrate than I thought."

She adjusted her body and her damn skirt slid up even farther.

She's your agent. You do not see sexy legs at all. Picture them with lots of hair!

Roger lifted the hose. "This may sting a little." He let the water trickle down her perfect thigh. After he was sure the small pieces of gravel were out of the wound, he took the bottom of his shirt and gently dried it as best as he could without causing her too much pain. He dropped the hose and turned off the water, then walked toward one of the plants between the boulders. "Hold on." He broke a piece of the plant off and walked back toward Sally with a spear about eight inches long.

She laughed. "You going to put me out of my misery now? I think you're taking this a little too far, don't you think? I'm going to live."

"This is aloe vera. One of the best things in the world. I'm just going to put a little bit on and you'll feel better." He squeezed some of the gooey aloe vera liquid out of the inside of the plant and on to his fingers and thumb. He applied some to the top of the wound. He grabbed the spear and squeezed more aloe vera out, this time rubbing it around the outside of the injured area.

"Where did you learn this? Don't tell me you used to be a Boy Scout?"

"I was MacGyver's apprentice." Roger winked and worked in a little more aloe vera around the outside of the wound. "How's this?"

Sally leaned back and closed her eyes. "That's good."

She moaned a few times and had the oddest grin on her face. What the hell was all that about? It was the same look she had that day he gave her that foot massage. This could be a while—no way he was going to stop now when he knew she enjoyed it so much.

As he rubbed her leg he gazed down to her feet. Her beautiful feet. Then his eyes traveled up to her shin, to the back part to admire the calf, and then moved up the knee. Next was her thigh, and then the slow finale all the way up her body to her eyes.

Her eyes that were open and watching him like a hawk.

Crap.

Her gaze dropped to his lips.

Man. The way she's looking at me.

Their eyes were locked and there was no way he could look away. He didn't want to look away. His breath got heavier and his hand forgot to move. It rested on her thigh. The woman would not look away. She had to be feeling what he was feeling. Rapid heartbeat. A stirring inside. His mind seemed to be going in a million directions but he couldn't piece together a cohesive thought. Well, except one.

Kiss that woman now.

He leaned closer. "Sally . . ."

She met him halfway. "Yes . . ."

She looked down at his mouth again and that was all he could take. He dropped the aloe vera stick and moved in for a kiss. First, a soft one. Just lips connected, almost frozen, like they just needed to touch and that would be good enough. He nibbled on her lower lip and she opened her mouth, letting him in. Their tongues danced together and he took the kiss deeper and deeper. This was the greatest kiss of his life and he didn't want it to end. Roger had forgotten the time, the day of the week, the month, the year, and where he was. And he was totally okay with that.

Let this kiss last forever.

"Excuse me!" called a voice, interrupting Roger's state of ecstasy. "What do you think you're doing?"

Roger pulled away from Sally's lips. She sat up and pulled her skirt back down. They both turned together toward the voice.

Mr, Crotchety

An older woman with white hair stood on the patio looking over the rim of her glasses. "I asked you a question."

Roger stood, took a few steps toward the woman. "It's not what you think. I'm Roger Hudson and I want to buy your house."

"Oh, do you?" Her eyes traveled to meet Sally's. "And this is your . . . wife?"

Sally stood up and adjusted her skirt a little more. "No. I'm Sally Bright. I'm his agent."

The woman's eyes darted back and forth between the two, then back to the lawn chair, and finally stopping on the ground beneath the chair. Roger and Sally followed her eyes.

"Did you butcher my aloe vera plant?" the woman asked. She walked over and picked up the aloe vera spear he had broken from the plant. "This is vandalism! Get off my property!"

Roger pointed to Sally. "She was injured and I was merely applying the aloe vera to the wound."

"With your tongue?"

"No, I had to—"

"Which office do you work for?"

Sally hesitated and then answered. "Big Basin Homes."

"Uh-huh. Well, listen here, I don't appreciate you coming onto my property and acting like a couple of horny teenagers. You can be sure I'm going to call your office and complain to the owner. Now get out of here."

"My client is interested in your property."

"Well, you can forget about it. I wouldn't sell it to you for ten million dollars. Please leave. And use the side gate."

Roger and Sally didn't say another word. They walked through the side yard to the driveway and got in Sally's car. They stared straight ahead through the windshield at the house as Sally started the engine. The car idled and Roger didn't like the silence. He wanted to hear Sally's laughter and her energetic personality. A couple of minutes later she was still speechless and he couldn't take it anymore.

He turned to her. "We need to talk about what happened."

She shook her head. "Maybe now isn't the best time."

"Now's the perfect time since it's fresh in our minds and —"

"Stop. I have a feeling I know what you're going to say, Roger, and I'm not going to be very happy when you *do* say it. Let's get something clear . . . I'm not a fool and I know we're attracted to each other. I don't know what happened in that backyard or what will be the result of what happened, but I wouldn't be surprised if you're scared or confused. You've been through a lot, I know. So have I! But we're adults and let's just have the confidence and the adventure to explore this and see where it goes."

"I—"

She held up her hand. "Don't tell me that kiss was a mistake and it should've never have happened. Because if you say it or even think it, you're one hundred percent wrong and I'll make you walk home."

Roger's smile turned into a chuckle.

Sally sighed. "I'm not kidding."

His chuckle turned into a full-blown laugh.

"Stop that and be honest with me. Were you going to tell me the kiss was a mistake?"

His smile faded. "You're not even close."

Sally studied Roger—probably wondering if he was lying. "Okay. What were you going to say then?"

"Thank you for asking. I was going to say we should both go home and get cleaned up because I would like to take you to dinner this evening."

Sally stared at him again. "Dinner?"

"Yes, dinner. It's that meal conveniently located between lunch and breakfast."

A smile formed on Sally's face. "Really?"

"Yes, really."

"I'd like that."

"Me, too."

She put the car in reverse and backed out of the driveway. Then she stepped on the brakes. "When you say dinner, are you talking about a business dinner or a—you know—a social dinner?"

"I'm taking you out on a date."

"Oh . . ."

"And as much as I look forward to getting to know you better, what I *really* look forward to is the end of the date where I hope to get another one of those fantastic kisses."

Sally stuck the car in park. "Why do you need to wait until then?"

A smile formed on Roger's face right before he kissed her again.

Chapter Thirteen

Sally shared another amazing kiss with Roger up in the hills above Saratoga before she dropped him off at his store. An hour later they were having dinner together. It was her first date since her divorce was final two years ago.

La Fondue was an experience for the senses and the palate. There must have been fifty different smells that fought for Sally's attention. Meats, seafood, veggies, cheeses, chocolate. So much going on in the air as she admired the dark wood walls and tables and the ornate gold-framed mirrors on the walls.

The restaurant had modern chandeliers encased in glass and each table had a warmer in the center for the fondue. She loved the retro, olive-colored velvet overstuffed chairs and sofas. The owners knew it was important to be comfortable while you stuffed your face.

She felt like a teenager out with the prom king. The man who sat across from her was changing right before her eyes, by the hour even. Mr. Crotchety was showing his true colors, not even close to crotchety. Roger had a soft and kind side, a warm heart, and a smile that made her heart dance. She loved that he was romantic, opening her car door for her, pulling out her chair for her, the whole shebang. And man, oh man, could he kiss. She would have never thought it the first time she laid eyes on him at Highway 9 Sandwiches. First impressions aren't always the right ones and sometimes the heart can see what the eyes are missing. Sally continued to stare across the table at the handsome man dressed in a black pinstriped button down shirt.

As if he knew she was looking at him Roger dropped the menu a few inches. "You have one of the most beautiful, authentic smiles I've ever seen. Don't ever stop doing that."

Compliments like that will get you everywhere! "Thank you, but I'm not sure I can smile while I'm sleeping. Or at the dentist. And I don't think I've *ever* smiled at the DMV."

Roger winked at her. "I bet you have." He reached across the table and grabbed her hands. "I'm going to admit something to you and I hope you won't laugh."

Roger's face got serious for a moment. His smile disappeared.

Sally squeezed his hands. "I won't laugh. I promise."

He leaned in a little closer to her. "I haven't been out on a date in five years. Since Macy died. This feels odd and wonderful and crazy and scary at the same time. But there's nowhere I would rather be, so please be patient with me."

She squeezed his hands again. "I promise."

Sally loved that he was able to admit something like that. His honesty and sincerity were refreshing and made her even more attracted to him.

"What about you?" he asked. "I know it's probably not a great idea to talk about past relationships, but have you dated much since your divorce?"

How did he know I was divorced?

"Sorry," he added. "Maggie told me you were divorced. And if you don't want to talk about any of that I completely understand. We can talk about whatever you want. I'm anxious to get to know you better."

"I don't mind. I got divorced two years ago and haven't dated since. Not that I didn't want to."

"Kids?"

She shook her head. "You?"

"We tried—it just wasn't in the cards. But you've met my nephew and he almost feels like a son to me."

"I like Jeffrey." Sally smiled. "Honestly, I was too focused on my career to think about anything else and that's what led to our marital problems."

"Your husband got tired of being home alone on the weekends?"

Sally chuckled. "Yeah, pretty much. Can't blame him either. But maybe if we'd had a stronger connection I would have cut back on work. I don't know. He was a kind person, don't get me wrong. Just not a lot of passion. Honestly, I should've seen that red flag the day he proposed."

"What did he do?"

"You don't want to know."

Sally wondered if now was a good time to tell Roger she

was a cancer survivor. She was curious how he'd take it considering his wife had died of cancer. She decided to wait —the first date wasn't the best moment to reveal something like that.

The waiter approached. "Here you go." He uncorked a bottle of Merlot and poured them both a glass. "You ready to order?"

Roger set his menu on the table. "Do you mind giving us a few more minutes?"

"Not at all."

As the waiter walked away Sally lifted her glass. "Cheers."

"Not so fast," said Roger. "I want to hear about your ex's passionless proposal."

"Seriously?"

"Seriously."

"It's bad."

"It's my turn to try not to laugh."

"Okay." Sally took a sip of her wine. "He bought a house and was remodeling it. The plan was we would live there together after we got married. Anyway, there was a trash dumpster on the street in front of the house and . . ." She took another sip of wine and swallowed. Then she burst in laughter. "It's so horrible it's funny. Okay, okay. He hung a banner on the dumpster in front of his house and then knelt down in front of the dumpster and asked me to marry him."

"He asked you to marry him in front of a trash

dumpster?"

"Yeah."

"What did the banner on the dumpster say?"

She blinked twice. "Our future home."

Roger's lips were shut tight and he looked like a trumpet player trying to blow into his instrument. His face was turning red. Then purple. He couldn't hold it and let out an explosive gasp followed by the loudest laugh ever. Heads in the restaurant all turned in their direction.

Sally waved her hand at him. "You said you wouldn't laugh!"

"I tried not to, but that was before I knew you were going to live happily ever after in a trash dumpster!"

Sally laughed and took another sip of wine. "Yeah, that was pretty bad. Hey, it's not like I was looking for a proposal on top of the Eiffel Tower. But I think the least a guy can do is put a little thought into it and make it special and romantic."

Roger raised his glass. "To romance."

Sally clinked his glass. "Cheers."

"And sweet kisses."

Sally was happy to toast to that too. "Cheers, again."

Roger's gaze dropped to her lips and she felt her heart rate kick up a notch.

The waiter returned and took their order. After he walked away Sally fidgeted in her chair.

"Uncle Roger, what are the chances?"

Sally was so distracted by the gorgeous man in front of her she hadn't even noticed Portia and Jeffrey had entered.

Roger turned and did a double take. "Wait a minute." Sally could see Roger's mind working overtime trying to analyze what was going on. He ran his hand through his hair and shook his head. "This is the cougar?"

Not good.

"Excuse me?" said Portia. "That's uncalled for. Look, I'm totally okay with you not wanting me to be your agent, but don't insult me. I have nothing but the best intentions with your nephew. And it's none of your business, anyway."

The hostess approached. "Do you want us to combine your tables?"

"No!" Roger and Portia said at the same time.

The hostess jumped back, startled. "No problem."

The woman walked away, leaving the four of them there in silence.

Sally cleared her throat. "Okay, let's settle down, everyone." She stood and hugged Portia. "Nice to see you."

"You too," said Portia, who threw Roger a take-that-and-stuff-it look.

Sally scooted closer to Jeffrey and hugged him. "We missed you the other night for the movie. You never came back."

Jeffrey shrugged. "The thesis got the best of me, but if it makes you feel any better I know how it ended."

Sally laughed. "Of course you do. Well, enjoy your

dinner."

"You, too."

They walked away and Sally sat back down and eyed Roger. She wasn't surprised by his reaction. He loved his nephew very much and was protective. A little too much so, considering Jeffrey was an adult.

Roger watched them walk to their table and grunted.

"Hey," said Sally. Roger didn't respond so she snapped her fingers in front of his face. "Let it go. He's an adult."

"Yeah." Roger took a gulp of his wine.

"And for the record, Portia is not a cougar."

"You don't know what she does away from your office."

"I certainly do. She's my best friend."

Roger didn't respond. He took a sip of his wine and swirled it around in his mouth before swallowing it. This just seemed weird. He was out with Sally. And his nephew was out with her best friend. He glanced over at his nephew's table. Jeffrey was in the middle of an animated conversation with Portia and they seemed to be enjoying themselves.

Sally leaned across the table and turned Roger's head so it was looking at her. "I'm over here."

"I know that."

"Typically on a date the man focuses on the woman he's with, like she's the only thing in the room. That gives her the warm fuzzies. I like the warm fuzzies."

"You're right, you're right." He grabbed her hands and kissed them. "Sorry, I'm out of practice."

"That's okay." She lifted her glass. "To practice."

Roger laughed and toasted.

The waiter returned with the fondue pot and placed it on the burner in front of them.

Roger grabbed the salt shaker and shook a little salt in the palm of his hand.

Sally cocked her head to the side. "I wouldn't do that if I were you. I'm sure the sauce is perfect the way it is. The shrimp just needs to simmer inside for a little bit."

Roger glanced down at the fondue pot. "I wasn't going to add salt."

"No?"

"To be honest, I don't have a clue why I put salt in my hand."

"Wow. You *are* out of practice."

"Yeah. Hey, I heard it was good luck if you toss salt over your shoulder." He lifted his hand.

"Wait!" she whispered. She leaned in and waved him in with her fingers.

He leaned in to meet her in the middle of the table. "Yes?"

"There are people seated directly behind you," she whispered. "You looking to start a fight?" She held out her palm. "Give me the salt."

Roger glanced down at her hand and let the salt fall from his palm to hers.

She reached under the table and brushed her hands off.

Fifteen minutes later Roger and Sally enjoyed their meal.

Sally pulled a piece of shrimp from the fondue pot and ate it. "This is wonderful." She wiped her mouth. "Okay, this is where we engage in small talk, Mr. Hudson."

"Right. Small talk. I can do that. I heard you were one of the top salespeople in Silicon Valley. Have you always been in sales?"

"When I was five years old I sold lemonade in my front yard and did very well. I sold the most Girl Scout cookies in California for five years in a row and one year I set the national record."

"You were a superstar." He smiled and grabbed a piece of shrimp from the fondue pot. "Tell me more."

"Okay. In high school I did two major fundraisers that helped pay for a trip to New York to attend a Brian Tracy sales conference. I learned so much about people, engaging with them, talking to them in a down-to-earth way and not always trying to sell. That week was an amazing experience and gave me the confidence to get my real estate license at the age of nineteen."

"I'm impressed. You always knew what you wanted and you went for it."

"Yes. And you?"

Roger took a sip of his wine and thought about it. "I

studied business management in college. I always knew I wanted to have my own company. To be my own boss. That way my success or failure depended on nobody else but myself. I sold shoes at Nordstrom for three years before I was promoted to manager. I only did that to learn as much as I could before opening my own store."

"Where did you go to college?"

"Santa Clara. That's where I met——" Roger took another sip of his wine. "Sorry. Probably not a good idea to talk about Macy."

"Why not? She was a part of your life and those memories will always be with you, right?"

He nodded. "She was my college sweetheart."

"That's wonderful that you had someone like her in your life. Tell me more, if you don't mind."

"She was an amazing woman. Compassionate, loving, beautiful. And she didn't take any crap from me."

Sally grinned. "A girl after my own heart."

Roger laughed. "I admit it feels odd talking about her with you, but at the same time it feels good. Thank you."

"I didn't do anything. I think it's important that a man and woman can talk about whatever is on their minds at any given time."

"I agree. So your turn. Tell me something I don't know."

Sally finished working on another shrimp and topped it off with a little bit of wine. "I did want to tell you something and I was going to wait, but I guess now would be a good time."

"You're pregnant."

Sally chuckled and stared down into her wine glass. "No, silly. You have to have sex in order for that to—" She took another sip of wine. "Okay, getting off track here. How did the subject of sex come up on a first date? This is awkward. Anyway, I'll just say it." She locked eyes with Roger. "I'm a cancer survivor."

Roger just stared at her. He hadn't expected *that*. Maybe something else about her ex-husband or her family or her last vacation. Or something about enjoying long walks on the beach and vacations to South America. Not cancer. Macy died of cancer and he was now on a date with someone who survived cancer. Was he the only person who would think this was weird? What if Sally had a relapse? He barely got through Macy's death and there was no way he could go through it again. This hit so close to him. Too close. It felt like his head was about to explode, he couldn't remember how to breathe. He knew he needed to respond but just couldn't come up with anything.

Say something you idiot! She's staring at you!

He swallowed hard. "Okay . . ."

"I'm sorry. I realize this came out of nowhere but it was important to tell you as soon as possible, because of your experience with cancer. And by the look on your face I can see this is hard for you. So . . . if you'd like to take me home —"

"What?" He swallowed hard. "No way!"

"I just thought that—"

"No, no, no. You're not going anywhere. I'm enjoying your company very much. I'm sorry for my reaction. What you told me *is* a lot to take in and please don't misread this. I'm grateful you survived. I'm grateful for anyone who survives." Now it made sense why she was always so happy and alive. He reached across the table, grabbed her hand and kissed it. "It would've been less awkward to talk about sex."

Sally laughed. "Maybe so."

"There's that beautiful smile. I'm sorry for my reaction. And thank you for telling me."

The waiter cleared the table and prepared the dessert fondue. Not too long after that they dipped strawberries and bananas in dark Godiva chocolate.

Sally moaned as she licked chocolate off her finger. "By the way, how did you get a reservation on such short notice? Sometimes it can take a week or two to get in here for dinner."

"One of the owners buys shoes from me and there's a slight possibility I may have offered her two free pairs of shoes in exchange for a table."

"Slight possibility?"

"Okay. A one hundred percent possibility."

Sally held out her wine glass for another toast. "Well done. You just bypassed my ex on the romance scale."

Roger clinked her glass. "It wasn't that difficult. Women

love shoes."

"Amen."

Roger glanced over at his nephew's table. Jeffrey and Portia still looked like they were enjoying themselves, smiling and laughing. Jeffrey reached across the table and fed food to Portia.

"Hey," said Sally. "Back over here. Leave them alone."

"You're not going to take my crap either, are you?"

"No, sir."

"Good. I need someone to keep me in line. But please understand that I do have to look now because they just stood up and are walking this way."

Sally swung around and Portia threw her a smile.

Roger glanced down at Jeffrey's hand. It was attached to Portia's.

What the hell?

Jeffrey placed his free hand on his uncle's shoulder. "I just wanted you to be the first to know that we're getting married."

"That is the most ridiculous—"

"I'm kidding!"

Jeffrey and Portia got a good laugh out of that and Sally joined in.

Roger didn't think it was so funny. He glanced down at their attached hands again. "You're holding hands."

"Yeah." Jeffrey smiled at Portia. "Feels great."

Portia pointed to the chocolate fondue on the table.

"That looks amazing but we were too full to have the dessert. Talk tomorrow?"

Sally nodded. "I'll call you in the morning."

"Sounds good."

Jeffrey squeezed his uncle's shoulder again. "I'll call you in the morning."

Sally and Portia laughed.

Roger glared at his nephew. "Not funny. By the way, how did you get a reservation?"

"I just used a trick out of my old uncle's playbook. I offered the owner a free pair of shoes."

"Just one pair? I gave her two!"

"What can I say? I'm a natural born businessman."

Roger grunted.

Chapter Fourteen

The next morning Sally's office manager, Phillip, poked his head into her office. "Can we talk?"

"Of course. Come in."

Sally didn't like the serious look on his face. Hopefully this was just a little chat about something in the industry like interest rates or the median price of homes.

Wishful thinking.

She was pretty sure it had to do with that woman up on Pierce Road. She probably called Phillip to inform him of her behavior yesterday with Roger in the yard.

Phillip sat in the chair in front of her desk. "I just got the most disturbing call."

"Oh? What happened?"

"At first I thought it was somebody pulling a prank. Her accusations were outrageous and I thought she sounded a little nuts, to be honest. But I still need to ask you as part of my responsibility as office manager—just to cover our asses." Sally nodded but didn't respond. "Did you take Roger Hudson to go see a house on Pierce Road yesterday?

"Yes."

Phillip scooted up on the edge of the chair. "Okay, here's

the deal. The owner of that home said she interrupted you and Roger in the backyard while you were trying to have sex on her patio furniture. She said she kicked you off her property and then spent the next twenty minutes scrubbing clean a particular lounge chair where the alleged *activity* took place."

Sally laughed. "Oh my God."

"I didn't believe her because I know you're not that type of person but, like I said . . . Just need to ask. So?"

"The truth is I fell in the woman's backyard and Roger was applying aloe vera to my leg where I had scraped it." She hiked up her skirt a couple of inches and showed the gauze that covered the scrape.

Phillip grimaced. "Ouch. You okay?"

"It's fine."

He stood and shook his head. "I knew that woman was crazy. Okay, thanks."

Sally blew out a deep breath as she watched Phillip walk down the hallway. Glad that turned out okay. Yes, she had withheld some info from Phillip, like the part where she enjoyed Roger's lips. But he didn't need to know about that.

Sally's cell rang and she pulled it from her purse. "Good morning."

"I kissed him!" screamed Portia.

Sally laughed. "That's all? Just one kiss?"

"Hey, I wouldn't have minded a little more, but I'm not a slut. I could have kissed him all night. Man, oh man. I'm serious, it was like heaven."

Sally knew exactly how Portia felt. Roger's kisses were out of this world. She'd like to get a few more of them today when she saw Roger.

As for Portia, she had mentioned to Roger she had good intentions with Jeffrey. Sally believed her one hundred percent, but she never explained what those intentions were.

"Portia?"

"Yeah."

"Jeffrey is going back to San Diego next month. How do you feel about that?"

"I haven't put much thought into it, to be honest. I'm just having fun. Nothing wrong with that, right?"

"No, but I know you. A couple of days of fun and you're in love. Then when he moves back to San Diego that won't be fun at all."

"Maybe I'll move to San Diego."

Sally held the phone away from her face to stare at it. Who was she talking to? "You can't be serious."

"Why not? I can sell houses anywhere. Look, I know it sounds crazy and I haven't made the decision to do something as bold as that, but I'm just saying I'm open to the possibility. Life is short."

"You're telling *me* that?"

"Exactly. You know better than anyone that anything can happen at any time. So I'm going to live my life. Just like you. Which brings us to you and Roger."

"What about me and Roger?"

"I watched you last night more than a few times and it looked like you were enjoying yourself."

"I was! I'm telling you, he's not who he seems."

"I've only seen the crotchety side."

"He's changing, I'm telling you. The next time you see him you won't even recognize the man."

"Right."

"I'm serious! He's probably giving someone a huge compliment right at this very moment."

"I've got hemorrhoids older than you," said Roger. He dusted off the glass shelf on the wall behind the register where he displayed the shoe polish.

"Is that supposed to impress me?" asked Jeffrey, vacuuming the floor. "And age has nothing to do with wisdom. You expect me to believe you've never made poor choices in your life as a *mature* adult?"

"I never said I hadn't. I'm just saying it makes no sense why you would want to go out with that woman. And you came home very late last night. Did you sleep with her?"

Jeffrey laughed. "You sound like Mom. Just because I'm out late everyone assumes I'm either getting drunk, doing drugs, having sex, or up to no good."

"You didn't answer the question."

"No sex." He grinned. "We did kiss, though."

"Don't tell me that!" Roger placed the feather duster under the counter and added a couple of shoes to the New Arrivals section.

Roger's mind drifted to Sally and her kisses. He had to admit the day before was an absolutely wonderful day. They had struck out on the house search, but the kisses and dinner with her more than made up for it. Today was a new day and it was time to get serious about finding a new place to live. Sally emailed Roger early this morning to let him know about the offers that had come in on his house late last night. One of them was an all-cash offer, which meant the deal could technically close within a few days. He and Sally would get together today to go over everything and to also go look at other houses for sale.

Jeffrey wound up the vacuum cord and smirked. "What time is your girlfriend going to be here?"

Roger shook his head. "Could you please not call her that?"

"You look like a couple to me." He pushed the vacuum to the back and returned. "In fact, I may have to move up that wedding date." He looked behind the counter and scratched his chin. "Where's my notebook?"

Roger grinned. "I have no idea."

"Seriously, Uncle Roger. That's not funny."

"You've said a few things I didn't think were very funny, either. And you didn't seem to care enough to stop."

"Okay, okay. I'll stop. Give me the notebook."

"Don't ever mention the word girlfriend or wedding."

"Fine, fine. Give it to me."

Roger opened the receipt drawer and pulled the notebook out from where he had hidden it under some papers. He handed it to Jeffrey.

Jeffrey kissed it and immediately opened it. He clicked his pen a few times and spoke as he wrote. "Displays of cruelty and threats to derail plans of graduate thesis which would result in—"

Roger lunged for the notebook as the door swung open.

"Morning, boys!" said The Mouth.

"Good morning, Maggie," said Jeffrey.

"I'd say it's a *great* morning since I heard Roger Dodger here got a couple of offers on his house."

How the hell did she find out?

The woman was a spy. She must have hacked into Roger's email. She couldn't be trusted.

"Sounds like you'll be moving soon," she added.

Roger logged into the computer, careful that Maggie couldn't see his password. "It's not that simple. I still need to find a house and we didn't have any luck yesterday."

"Oh. I thought you were celebrating the new house last night at La Fondue. I was misinformed." Maggie frowned. "What are you looking for? I'm sure I can help you find a new house."

"Thanks, but that's why I hired Sally. She's a professional

and I'm going to let her do her job."

Maggie's phone rang and she pulled it from her purse. "I need to take this." She walked outside and a second later Sally entered.

"What a beautiful day!"

Roger froze.

Kiss? Hug? Handshake?

He wasn't sure what to do. He had the urge to kiss Sally, but she came to his place of business. Was he allowed to kiss her there? Were they out in the open about their relationship yet or were people supposed to keep it more discreet during business hours? Maggie would find out either way, but Jeffrey was there. He knew his nephew would have a field day with his notebook if he saw his uncle plant a wet one on the beautiful Sally Bright. Roger was stuck in limbo land.

Sally approached Roger. "You don't look so hot."

Kiss? Hug? Handshake? Do something!

Roger's hand shot out and hung in the air for Sally. "Nice to see you."

She glanced down at his hand. "Seriously? You want to shake my hand?"

Uh-oh. Wrong choice.

He pulled his hand back and wiped it on his pants. Then he leaned forward and tried to hug her but she jumped back out of his way.

Wrong again? Geez, Louise.

He lunged forward to kiss her and bumped heads with

Sally. Both of them grabbed their heads as the shelf of summer sandals went tumbling to the floor.

Jeffrey feverishly scribbled in his notebook and little bits of air were forced out of his tight mouth as he tried to hold in the laughter.

Roger put the shelf back in its place and picked up the sandals. "I'm really messing this up. I don't know why I'm so nervous."

Sally stepped forward and kissed Roger on the lips. She held the kiss there for a few seconds and then smiled. "You're a disaster. It's kind of cute but I think I may need some Tylenol or something."

He reached out and caressed her cheek. "Sorry."

"No need to apologize. Did you have a chance to look over the offers?"

"Yes."

"And?"

"They look good but I would like to find a house before I accept one of them."

"That's fine, but keep in mind both of the offers expire in forty-eight hours. Sorry. Hi, Jeffrey." She leaned in and hugged him. "Did you enjoy your dinner with Portia?"

Jeffrey grinned. "She rocks."

Sally laughed. "I agree." She turned back to Roger. "Ready to go? I have three more houses lined up for today."

Roger grabbed his cell phone from the counter and followed Sally out. "I hope the Fuscos' house is one of them."

"Unfortunately not. I'm not sure what's going on with that house, but I've left a message with the agent."

The more Roger thought about it the more he was interested in the Fuscos' home. Maybe the best thing to do would be to stop by their place and have a little chat with them in person.

Chapter Fifteen

Guilt shot through Sally again. She didn't like that Roger had mentioned the Fuscos' house again. She wanted to tell him the truth. It was eating her up. But what would happen if she told him she wanted that house for herself? Would he let her buy it? Or would he fire her on the spot and buy the house for himself?

Roger got in the passenger side of Sally's car and glanced down at her legs.

"Eyes on the road, Mr. Hudson."

He turned his attention to the street in front of them as Sally drove down Big Basin Way. "I can't get away with anything with you. It's okay for us to kiss in public but I can't look at your legs? Something's wrong with this picture."

Sally laughed. "Speaking of wrong, my manager Phillip came into my office today. He got a call from that woman up on Pierce Road. She said we were trying to have sex in her backyard yesterday."

Roger laughed. "What did Phillip say?"

"Well, lucky for us the woman exaggerated. If she had said we were kissing he might have suspected something. But he knew I wasn't the type of person to have sex in public so he dismissed her as a lunatic."

"You don't like sex in public?"

"Of course not."

"Damn. Remind me to cancel that picnic I had planned for us tomorrow." Roger tried to keep a straight face but was doing a horrible job of it.

Sally burst out in laughter. "You're crazy."

"And *you* are beautiful."

Five minutes later Sally pulled up in front of a two story colonial style brick house. It looked majestic from the street. A gardener pushed a mower across the front lawn.

"Sorry," said Roger. He stared out the window. "I should've told you but I've changed my mind."

"About what?"

"Two-story houses. I consider myself to be in excellent shape but it's probably not a wise idea to buy a two-story house at my age. People fall and break their hips and I certainly don't want to go through that."

"I think most people who break their hips are in their eighties and nineties."

"Time flies and I'll be there before you know it."

"Okay." Sally grabbed her list of houses from the folder in between the two seats and crossed the first house off the list. "Fortunately the next house on the list is just around the corner, so we haven't wasted much time."

"Good."

Two minutes later Sally parked in front of the second

house on the list. A four bedroom, three bath house at the end of a court.

Roger pointed to the cemented area on the side of the driveway. "A basketball court. I *love* that."

"You don't make any sense. You tell me you're afraid of breaking your hip from going up and down stairs at a slow pace, but then you're perfectly okay playing a physical sport where you can do even more damage?"

"What's so physical about playing Horse?"

Sally did a double take. "Horse?" It was one of her favorite games as a teenager.

"Yeah. It's been a long time since I've played but I was pretty good back in my day."

Sally grinned. "Me, too."

"I don't believe it."

She spotted the ball on the ground near the hoop and gestured to it. "The best."

He followed her eyes to the ball and grinned. "You're going to have to prove it because I still don't believe it."

The next thing they knew, instead of touring the house, Roger and Sally played Horse on the basketball court. It was the most fun she'd had in a long time. Roger wasn't joking, he was good. But he sure looked surprised every time she matched his shot. After Roger finally missed a shot from the free throw line Sally sank hers. Nothing but net.

"Yes!" she said. "If you miss this I win."

"What? We're not playing a full game?"

"We need to find you a house. Take the shot and miss it so I can win and gloat."

"Dream on. I've made this shot a thousand times." He threw the ball up and it hit the front of the rim. It bounced off the backboard and did a circle around the rim before it fell to the ground.

Sally threw her arms in the air. "I am the champion, my friend."

Roger laughed. "That's not how the song goes." He grabbed her around her waist and lifted her in the air. She screamed as he spun her around.

"Put me down!"

"As you wish."

He lowered her and her body rubbed against his on the way down. He looked in her eyes and pulled her in for a kiss. Another amazing kiss.

"What's going on here?" called a voice from the car that pulled into the driveway.

Roger and Sally turned around.

Not again.

The man got out of the car and grabbed the basketball from the ground. He tossed it behind him on the lawn. "This isn't a public park. Please leave."

Sally stepped forward to address him. "Sorry. My name is Sally Bright and I'm a real estate agent. We're here because I'm showing my client your property."

The man eyed Roger. "Your client?"

"Yes."

Roger stepped forward. "I'm Roger Hudson. You've got a great property here. I like what I see."

The man glanced back over to Sally. "You've been inside?"

Sally shook her head. "We were just getting ready to go in."

"After you were done playing make out? Do you realize how unprofessional this is?"

Sally pointed to the basketball court. "Roger wanted to test the court."

"What office do you work for?"

"Big Basin Homes."

Sally picked up her purse from the ground and pulled a business card out. She didn't want to give the man the card, but she didn't have a say in the matter. You visit a house, you leave a business card. That was the protocol.

He inspected the business card. "Good day." He walked toward the front door.

Sally took a few steps toward the house and tried to stop the man. "Excuse me . . ."

The man stopped and turned around, eyeing Sally but not answering.

"We still would like to see the house inside. As my client said, he likes what he sees and—"

"I'm going to call your office and file a complaint against you."

Roger took a few steps forward and raised his palms. "We were just shooting some hoops. Lighten up."

The man just stared at Roger.

Sally pulled Roger by the arm. "It's okay. Let's go."

They were silent in the car for a few minutes as Sally drove to the next house around the corner.

Roger sighed. "That guy sure was crotchety."

Sally shot Roger a look and laughed.

A few seconds later Roger laughed with her.

She was having so much fun with Roger and wanted to skip work today. But she knew how important it was for Roger to find a house. She drove down Cox Avenue across the railroad tracks and passed the fire station.

After she made a left on Seagull Way Roger slapped the dashboard. "Oh, wow. Turn right here!"

"Why?"

She had a feeling she knew why and didn't like the sick feeling in her stomach. "We have one more house to see. Let's stick with the plan."

"Turn!"

Sally didn't turn. Instead she pulled over and stuck the car in park. "What's going on?"

"I just want you to turn right here on Yuba Court and go to the end. I want to see the Fuscos' house again. I haven't been by here in a while and want to see if anything has changed."

What lie are you going to come up with this time?

"Sally?"

"Uh . . . they're having the place fumigated, so right now the home looks like a giant circus tent. You won't be able to see a thing."

"Oh. Okay, that's too bad." He was deep in thought for a few moments. "Well, can you at least get them on the phone so we can talk to them?"

Sally shook her head. "They went out of town since they couldn't stay in the house while the work was done. I can let you know when they return."

She sat there for a moment and thought about the hole she had dug herself into. It was getting deeper and deeper. Portia was right. She just needed to come clean and hope Roger wouldn't want the house.

The truth shall set you free!

Or not. Maybe the truth would make her lose her dream house. Or maybe she'd lose Roger. Or both. She just needed to stick to the plan and find him a house so nice he wouldn't care anymore about the Fuscos' property.

"Sally?" said Roger. "What's on your mind?"

"Well . . ." She thought about it a little more but couldn't pull the trigger. "I was just thinking what a beautiful day it was."

And with each lie she felt guiltier.

Chapter Sixteen

Later that afternoon Sally returned to her office after dropping off Roger back at his store. He liked the last property that was located near Saratoga Country Club but she had found out while she was there the owner had accepted an offer from someone else. The agent just hadn't updated the MLS system yet. It was back to square one.

The good news was Roger had accepted the cash offer on his house and the closing date would be in only two days. That's also when the Fuscos' property would hit the market. Now she just had to quickly find him a house. She hated lying to Roger and was certain she was going to get an ulcer out of this.

Portia entered Sally's office and plopped down in the chair. "Just confirmed I'm going out with Jeffrey again this evening."

"Date number two! This is getting serious. What's the plan?"

"He's going to surprise me. He said to make sure I'm hungry and to bring a jacket, just in case."

"Sounds like something in the great outdoors. Alaska, maybe?"

"That's very realistic. And you and Mr . . . uh, Roger? Any plans?"

"Not sure yet but he did accept the cash offer on his house. It closes in two days, exactly when the Fuscos' house goes live."

Portia screamed. "I'm so happy for you!" She ran around the desk and hugged Sally. "And the wedding date? Did you pick one out yet?"

Sally pursed her lips. "Don't start."

Portia laughed. "Okay, but I should tell you that Jeffrey predicted the two of you would be married within three months. He even told Roger this."

"Roger and me married?"

Sally knew she had strong feelings for the man, but marriage? Would she go through it all over again? She wasn't sure why she even asked herself that question because the answer would definitely be yes.

A horrifying thought just crossed Sally's mind. "Oh, no."

"What?"

Sally popped up from her chair and looked out the window. "I didn't think this through very well. Not at all."

Portia got up and joined her at the window, looking out. "You don't like where you parked?"

Sally turned back to her desk and sat on the edge of it. "Listen, this is a big problem. I admit I can picture Roger and me getting very serious—I have a good feeling about it. But he's buying a new home."

"And"

"So am I."

"*And?*"

Sally sighed. "Which house would we live in? I don't want to go through this to buy my dream house only to have him tell me I need to live with him in his."

"Ahhh. I understand." Portia sat on the edge of the desk next to Sally. "I don't think that's your biggest problem, though."

"No?"

Portia shook her head. "Your problem is how you're going to explain that *you* bought a house that *he* was interested in *while* you were going out with him and never managed to mention a single word about it even once." She grimaced. "I have to say this is getting pretty hairy now that I think about it. How many lies have you told?"

"A couple."

Portia just stared at her.

"Okay, maybe a few more. Five. Six. Seven. But they were all the same lie, so technically it's just one."

"If you had two hundred cans of tuna in your shopping cart do you think you'd be allowed to go through the fifteen-items-or-less-express lane at Safeway just because they're all the same item?"

"You lost me."

"Never mind. You're screwed."

"Help me out of this! I don't want to lose the house and

I don't want to lose Roger."

Portia paced back and forth in Sally's office and rubbed her chin. A few seconds later she sat on the edge of the desk again, lighting up.

Sally lunged toward her. "What? Tell me!"

"Okay, I think this should work but it'll take some luck, timing, and quite possibly some or a lot of persuading on your part. You need to find Roger the perfect house *today*. Not tomorrow. Find one that's vacant and ready to move in to. Broaden the search to include houses just above his price range. If it's the perfect house and only ten percent higher in price, he's not going to say no. After you find Roger the house and he makes an offer, casually mention the Fuscos' house was finally put on the market. Then, casually mention that since *he* didn't get a chance to buy it, *you* might as well, since it's such a nice house. He'll be very happy with the purchase he made and would care less by then. And you both will live happily ever after. The end."

"Not really. Because if we're going to live happily ever after it would have to be in the same house."

"*Yes*, but you both love the Fuscos' house, so he would just have to sell the other one or rent it out. No big deal. I think my plan's a pretty good one."

"Yeah." Sally nodded and thought about it. "I think it'll work. It's my only option anyway, so what have I got to lose? I certainly don't want to lose Roger over this."

"I agree. And no more lying. It's not you."

Phillip poked his head in Sally's office again. "Knock, knock."

Oh, no. Did he hear that?

Portia jumped up from the edge of the desk. "I was just leaving."

Sally sat back in her chair. "What's going on?"

Phillip sat in the chair and didn't answer. He ran his fingers through his hair. It looked like there was a ping pong match going on inside of his mouth the way his tongue went back and forth, banging against each cheek. He was obviously there to talk about the incident at that home with the basketball court. It was crazy and romantic, but now she was going to suffer the consequences.

Good luck getting out of this one.

Sally pushed her laptop aside and forced a smile. "Anything in particular you wanted to talk about?"

"Yeah . . ." He moved his butt around in her chair and tried to find a better position. "Oddly enough, I just got *another* disturbing call regarding you and Roger. I dismissed the first call as nonsense because I thought I knew you well enough, but when the second call came in I wondered what was really going on here. Two calls from two completely different people isn't a coincidence. Is there something you want to tell me?"

"The man with the basketball court?"

Phillip nodded. "He said you were trespassing. He also said you and Roger were playing some form of dirty-dancing-basketball, which ended with a game of tongue hockey. Sally, what the hell is going on?"

What the hell *was* going on? That was a good question. This wasn't how a fifty-year-old woman acted.

Tell him the truth.

"It's true—what the man said. I'm sorry. I took Roger there to look at the house. We saw the basketball court and started playing Horse. One thing led to another—I kicked his butt, by the way—and the next thing I know we were kissing. I don't know what came over us and it won't happen again. We did go there to look at the house. Really."

Phillip leaned closer. "You were playing Horse?"

"Yeah. I love Horse. Used to play it as a kid."

"Me, too." Phillip cleared his throat. "And the sex on the patio furniture incident yesterday?"

"Did *not* happen!"

"Okay, okay. So do me this favor then. It sounds like you and Roger have something going on and I'm *totally* okay with that. But can you try to maintain some type of professional behavior when you're out representing this office? I don't want to receive another call about you and Roger at a property in some compromising position."

"Absolutely. I'm sorry, Phillip. It won't happen again."

"Good. And . . . I'm glad to see you're having fun after all you've been through. You deserve it."

"Thank you."

That was sweet of him to say. And Sally agreed. She did

deserve it.

But enough fun for now. She had to find Roger a house. She logged into the MLS system and did a new search with Roger's preferences. She filtered the results so it only showed homes that were vacant and she upped the price limit ten percent. She wasn't sure what would come up in the search since the real estate market was so hot and everything sold quickly. But after she expanded the criteria for price, she had found it. The perfect house for Roger.

Now all she had to do was convince him to buy it.

Roger placed the box of shoes and the receipt in the bag and handed it to the woman. "Thanks for coming in."

"Thank you!" she said.

After she left Roger whistled as he placed his copy of the receipt in the drawer. "A big day in sales today."

Jeffrey grinned. "Not that big of a surprise."

"Sure it is. Almost triple what we had last week."

"I know that. And I also knew today would be a great day before it happened. I have it documented if you'd like to see my notes." Jeffrey reached for his notebook.

Roger slapped his hand. "Not necessary. What are you trying to say? You can predict the future?"

"Yes, but not in the way you think. I'm not psychic, of course. I predicted it based on human behavior. *Your* human behavior."

"Oh. That."

"Sales are up three hundred percent over the last few days and it's all because of the energy you're emitting."

"You make me sound like a car. I have emissions now? That's ridiculous. There are always peaks in the sales cycle. Summer brings out a lot of people who are on vacation, people who want new shoes for hiking, new sandals for the beach. That has nothing to do with my behavior and everything to do with people motivated to do things in the summer."

"Last week was summer. And the week before. How come sales weren't up during those weeks? Look, I'm just saying people are more prone to buy things when they're in the right frame of mind. And their frame of mind can be *altered* by the way *you* treat them when they come in through that door. Even by the music you play on the sound system in the store. Which reminds me, you need to get a sound system in here and cater the music to the demographic most likely to buy the types of shoes you carry. Studies have shown people are more likely to make a purchase when they hear a song they love while they're shopping."

"Hopefully it's not too late and you can get a refund on that education of yours."

Jeffrey laughed. "You know I'm right."

There was something to Jeffrey's theory, but Roger certainly wasn't going to admit it. At least, not yet. This week had been amazing but the sales had nothing to do with it. Roger couldn't get his mind off of Sally. Day and night, she was all he thought about. He looked forward to seeing her later.

Jeffrey pointed to Roger's face. "You're smiling."

Roger made his smile disappear. "No, I'm not."

After he adjusted a few shoes on the shelf Jeffrey straightened out one of the chairs. "Can I leave early today? I've got a hot date and need to prepare."

"No."

"Are you denying me because you need me to do something here or because you still disapprove of me going out with Portia?"

"Both."

"Ha! I didn't expect that answer. Okay, what do you need me to do?"

Roger wasn't surprised that Jeffrey didn't put up a fight and try to get out of helping out. His nephew had a big heart and was such a loving person. He really didn't need Jeffrey to do anything at all. And he wasn't going to make something up just so he couldn't go on the date. No way he could ever lie to someone he cared about. He just said that to torture his nephew a little. He just had to let Jeffrey go do his thing and hope for the best.

"I don't need you to do anything for me. Go. Have fun."

"Thank you." Jeffrey hugged Roger. "Man, you've changed in such a short time since I've arrived. I'd like to take the credit but you and I both know it's because of Sally. It's good to see you smile again and explore your feelings with the other sex."

"Feelings, shmeelings." Roger gave him a look. "Get out of here before I change my mind."

"Ha! Nice try. It's obvious you care for Sally. Anyone can see that. But I'll drop the subject before you make me clean the toilet."

"Smart man. Take Crouton home with you."

"You got it." Jeffrey attached the leash to Crouton's collar and left.

Roger didn't admit it, but his nephew was right. He had strong feelings for Sally. The last time his feelings were this strong for someone was right before he told Macy he loved her for the first time. There was no doubt he was going in that direction with Sally. He could feel it in his gut. And in his heart.

Roger grabbed his ringing cell phone from the counter and checked the caller ID.

Sally.

"You knew I was thinking about you?" he said, after answering.

Sally laughed. "We have those infamous intuitions that men don't have, you know?"

"Believe me, I know."

They shared a laugh together. It felt wonderful.

"I found the perfect house for you and we have to go see

it before someone else buys it. Are you free right now?"

"Jeffrey just left, so I need to stay and close up the shop. I can be ready to go in about thirty minutes."

"Great. I'll come pick you up there."

"Wait. How are you so sure I'm going to love this house? Is it because it's the Fuscos' house?" There was silence on the other end of the line. "Sally?"

"No, it's not the Fuscos' house. It's even better."

"Better? This I gotta see."

"You're going to fall in love with this house."

Not before I fall in love with you.

Chapter Seventeen

Sally arrived at Roger's store just as he was getting ready to set the alarm. He opened the door and stuck his head out. "I'll be right there. Give me one minute."

"I'll give you two."

He smiled. "So kind . . ." Roger closed the door, grabbed his cell phone and keys, and then punched in the password on the wall unit to set the alarm. As the intermittent beeps sounded he headed outside and locked the front door behind him. "Okay. Ready."

He took a few steps toward Sally's car and she cleared her throat. "We're not taking my car."

Roger grinned. "I get to drive?"

"No. We're walking."

Roger stared down the street. "The house is that close?"

"Just around the corner. Come on."

This caught Roger by surprise. As they walked he imagined what it would be like to live so close to work you could walk there every single day. He loved the idea. Now he just had to love the house. They walked down Big Basin Way to the 76 Gas Station and made a left. Then they made another left down a quiet tree-lined street. But something didn't feel right. Not about the street. About Sally.

Roger reached over and grabbed her hand. "How come so quiet?" He pulled her to a stop and locked eyes with her. "Everything okay?"

She reached up and kissed him on the lips. "Of course. Sorry, I'm just anxious to show you the house."

He smiled. "I'm anxious to see it."

They walked past a few more houses and Sally stopped. She pointed to the yellow house with the tile roof in front of them. Well, not really yellow. More like a toasted sunflower. It looked like something you'd see maybe in Spain or another part of Europe, not Saratoga. It was gorgeous. The yard was well-manicured with a small lawn and a few Japanese maple trees. And he loved the circular driveway.

"Well?" she said. "What do you think so far?"

He clapped his hands together. "Love it."

"How did I know you were going to say that?"

"Because the only thing that exceeds your beauty is your intelligence."

"I'm so tempted to kiss you again, but we're on private property and that usually gets us into trouble. Which reminds me—Phil gave me a warning about my behavior while showing houses so keep your hands to yourself while we're inside."

"Yes, ma'am. It's not going to be easy, though."

She opened the lock box that hung from the front door and pulled the house key out.

They entered and Sally pointed to the floor. "Formal tile entryway." She closed the door behind them and led Roger to the kitchen, from there to the family room, and then the master bedroom with vaulted ceiling. It was a four bedroom home with three bathrooms and the more they walked through it, the more Roger liked it.

"This is a gorgeous home."

"But wait, there's more." Sally led Roger to the last room at the far end of the other hallway. Roger stepped inside and turned his head to the side.

What the hell?

He stuck his head back out into the hallway and stared down toward the other end where the master bedroom suite was. It didn't make any sense. "Okay, I'm having a déjà vu here."

Sally laughed. "Two identical master bedroom suites on opposite ends of the house. And here was my idea—this one has less light than the other one because of the trees out back, so this could be your movie theater." She pointed to the wall on the right. "Plenty of room for the popcorn machine, candy counter, chairs, everything. Even a bathroom!" Then she looked up. "And since it has the vaulted ceiling you can still do the art deco."

Roger nodded but didn't speak. He was impressed. Sally nailed it with this one. He was completely sold. She didn't have to say another word.

"And one more thing . . ." She walked down the hallway.

He moved faster to catch up with her. "There's more?"

"Of course! The backyard."

She unlocked the sliding glass door that went to the backyard and slid it open. Sally and Roger stepped outside and he froze.

So much privacy. So much nature. So much green.

What's that sound?

"Don't tell me . . ." He walked straight across the lawn to the end of the yard and looked down the embankment. "Well, I'll be a . . ."

He stared down at the flowing water of Saratoga Creek. He would have a creek in his backyard. Unbelievable.

He turned back to Sally, who was smiling. He walked toward her, not able to contain the grin on his face. He grabbed her by the waist and pulled her in for a hug. Then he lifted her off the ground and spun her around.

She screamed but held on to him tight. "Put me down, Roger. Remember? Hands off!"

He laughed and set her down. "Fine. No hands." He leaned down and kissed her on the lips. Not a peck. A good kiss.

Sally pulled away from the kiss and patted him on the chest. "Okay, okay, tiger." She adjusted her dress and looked around the property. "Another five-star kiss indeed, but we need to control ourselves. We're here strictly on business and I've been warned by Phillip." She smiled. "I take it by your response you like the place?"

He grinned. "Let's make an offer."

"Let's? You mean *you* are going to make an offer."

"Right. Me. But you like the place, right?"

"Of course. This house is gorgeous."

"Good. Because I picture you spending a lot of time here in the future."

Sally couldn't believe Portia's plan had worked. Even better, Roger had hinted that they would be seeing a lot of each other in the future. This was getting serious, no doubt. It felt wonderful, but she felt conflicted. She'd always wanted the Fuscos' house, but did it matter now? It didn't seem so. Maybe the wise choice would be to give up the dream of owning that house. Because when all is said and done, a house is just a house. It doesn't make your life.

They walked back to her car and Roger got in. Sally drove straight to her office to take care of the paperwork for the offer. She had started a generic offer before she'd met Roger today, so now all she had to do was fill in a little more info and have him sign it so she could send it over to the seller's agent.

Roger sat across from her at her desk as she finished the final details on the document. A growl rumbled from Sally's body and she dropped her hand over her stomach.

Roger grinned. "Someone's hungry."

"Starving. I'm almost done, then we can go grab a bite."

A little over an hour later the offer was done and Sally emailed it to the seller's agent. Then she left a voicemail for the agent to confirm it was received.

"Done!" said Sally, hanging up the phone.

"Time to celebrate," said Roger.

"Sounds wonderful. Do you want to include Jeffrey in on the celebration?"

"He's supposed to be having dinner with your best friend this evening."

"You could always ask them to join us. I mean, you need to get over that. They're both adults, you know?"

He crinkled his nose. "Yeah, I know." Roger texted Jeffrey and found out they were just walking into Bella Saratoga, a great Italian place not too far from Sally's office.

Sally and Roger walked there from her office and joined Jeffrey and Portia, who had grabbed a table for four.

Jeffrey stood and hugged Roger. "Congratulations, Uncle Roger. I'm so excited for you."

"Yeah, well your excitement level might change since you're going to help me move."

"Odd, but you're right. My enthusiasm has somewhat diminished."

They all laughed, took their seats, and ordered.

After the wine arrived Jeffrey held out his glass. "To your new house."

Everyone said together, "Cheers."

Roger took a sip of his wine and then held his glass back out over the middle of the table. "And to Sally. Thank you for helping me sell my home and for helping me find a new one. And above all, thanks for being patient with me while I was being a jackass."

"Cheers," they all said.

"And now that I think about it." Roger held out his glass again. "A toast to Portia for putting up with my jackass-ness too. Is that a word? Anyway, you get the idea. I apologize for my behavior."

Portia smiled and clinked his glass. "Apology accepted." She took a sip of her wine and shook her head. "It's amazing —you're a completely different person. Sally has rubbed off on you."

Roger reached under the table and squeezed Sally's hand. "You got that right."

And with that sweet caress she'd made a decision. This wonderful man was more important than any house. Enough was enough. What she had done was wrong. She was going to confess she'd been lying about the Fuscos' house because she wanted to buy it for herself. And if he still wanted the house she would do whatever she could to make it happen. No more stress. No more lies. Tomorrow, though. She wasn't about to ruin a perfect evening with her confession. She'd tell Roger everything in the morning.

Mr, Crotchety

It was a wonderful celebration at Bella Saratoga and Roger was on top of the world. It was a great idea to have Jeffrey and Portia there to celebrate. Roger had to admit that Portia was a good catch and he'd misjudged her. He wouldn't be surprised if Jeffrey and Portia ended up together somehow.

Speaking of being together, Roger was ready to take his relationship with Sally to the next level. Tomorrow he would ask her to go away with him to Napa for the weekend. It would be a great little romantic getaway for just the two of them. She was a very special woman and he felt grateful to have met her. Then he would have to come back and get serious about moving. Funny how things changed so quickly. It wasn't that long ago when he thought she was an annoying woman.

After dinner, Roger walked Sally back to her office to get her car. She offered to drop him off back at the shoe store, but he preferred to get some fresh air and try to work off some of that huge meal he had just eaten. He kissed her goodnight and headed down Big Basin Way toward the store. He looked forward to seeing Sally again tomorrow and just the thought put a little kick in his step, which hopefully burned a few calories, too.

He approached Carol's Antique Gallery and admired the two people staring at an old figurine in the window. They were an older white-haired couple holding hands.

Very sweet.

He passed them and wondered if he would be holding Sally's hands at that age. He was confident the answer was yes.

"Roger?" called out a voice from behind him.

He turned around and froze. It was William and Tammy Fusco. *They* were the couple holding hands.

How could that be?

"William, Tammy," said Roger. "What a surprise. I thought you were out of town."

William squished his white eyebrows together. "Why would we go out of town when we're moving? The movers just packed up everything and the house is empty. We're staying in a hotel tonight and leave for Palm Springs in the morning."

Roger scratched his head. "I guess I was misinformed. I was told you went out of town while your house was being fumigated for termites."

"We haven't had termites since the eighties!"

Roger felt his heart rate kick up a notch. He didn't like the direction of this conversation and he had a feeling he knew the answer to the next question, but he had to ask it anyway. "Did your agent get a call from my agent saying I was interested in your property?"

"No."

"You've got to be kidding me."

"Not at all." William placed his hand on Roger's shoulder. "But it's not too late if you're still interested."

Roger wanted to get drunk. All of those warm wonderful feelings about Sally were fading away in an instant. They were replaced with anger, confusion, and sadness. Why would Sally have lied to him about the house? And what else had she lied about?

Roger shook his head. "That's just it. I was given bad information by my agent about the status of your house, so I made an offer on another house. Just this evening, in fact."

"That's a shame," said Tammy. "Who's your agent?"

"Sally Bright."

Her eyes widened. "Oh, boy."

"What?" asked Roger.

William frowned. "Our agent told us Sally was interested in our home. For herself."

Roger felt like he'd been smacked in the head with a two by four. Any energy he had left was sucked from his body. He'd been betrayed by the woman he was falling in love with. He placed his hand on his heart. He wanted to look inside his chest to see how many pieces it was broken into. He tried to replay the different conversations he'd had with Sally in his mind but he just couldn't piece things together. Just minutes earlier he'd been on top of the world.

Now he was numb.

How could Sally be so cruel? How could she lie to him? Did she use him for his money? For the commission? He completely misjudged her. In fact, he had no idea who that woman was.

Roger said goodbye to the Fuscos and continued down the street. He stopped in front of Rose International Market, not being able to take it anymore. He wanted to explode. He pulled the cell phone from his pocket and called Sally. The only thing he wanted was for her to come clean. Admit the lies. The deceit. He'd at least give her this opportunity.

She picked up on the first ring. "Miss me already?"

"Yes."

"That's sweet. Thanks again for dinner. I had a wonderful time."

How do I know you're not lying? You're very good at it.

"Roger?"

"Do you know who did the termite work for the Fuscos?"

There was silence on the other end of the line.

"Pardon me?" said Sally.

"The Fuscos. You said they were having their house fumigated, right?"

"Uh…Yeah."

"So, I'd like to know if you know *who* was doing the work for them."

"I don't know . . ."

"Of course not. Okay, then. I'm going to tell *you* who was doing the termite work for the Fuscos. Ready? The answer is . . . absolutely nobody! And how do I know this? Because I just ran into William and Tammy on the way back to the store. Which is odd, because you told me they were out of town! What do you have to say about that?"

More silence. While he waited for her to respond his body quivered with hurt. The more he listened to the silence on the phone, the more his heart broke. He shook his head in disgust. He finally let a woman back into his life after Macy, and look where it had gotten him. He should've just stayed bundled up in his little bitter cocoon. He was safe there. He was in control there. Now his life was spinning out of control. Again.

A few seconds later Sally let out a deep breath. "Roger . . ."

"Don't *Roger* me. I want you to withdraw the offer on that house. Right now."

"What? No! You can't do that. Listen to me, you'll lose the deposit."

"First of all, they haven't even accepted the offer yet. So call them and tell them I've changed my mind. If it's too late, so be it. I'll eat the deposit—I don't give a crap."

"You're overreacting. Just take some time to calm down and think this through. It's not worth losing the house over."

"That's all you care about? The house and the commission?"

"No! But you were talking about withdrawing the offer and as your agent it's my responsibility to—"

"Ha! I release you from all of your responsibilities. You're fired."

Chapter Eighteen

Two weeks later

Sally still hadn't had a good night's sleep. The words "You're fired!" bounced around in her head. All day. All night. Sure, she could distract herself occasionally with work, but whenever she had to drive by Roger's store or his home, it took every bit of effort to hold it together until she got back to the office. Then she would bawl like a baby in the bathroom. She couldn't even wear the shoes she had bought from him. They were tucked away in the back of her closet.

She loved Roger with all her heart. And she was lonely. Yes, she had a great friend in Portia who was always there for her, but she had grown attached to Roger. He was a good person. His Mr. Crotchety persona was just a cover. She knew the real Roger. A kind man with the heart of gold. And she had hurt that wonderful man by lying to him.

What a fool.

She missed the way he looked at her. His smile. His kisses. Nobody had ever kissed her like that. She wanted more but she wasn't going to get it. Nope. She had blown it. No Roger. No Fusco house.

At least Roger had been able to buy the house from William and Tammy. He'd already moved in, too. And he hadn't lost the deposit from the first house, which was a good thing. Sally's manager Phillip had stepped in to finish the last bit of details from the sale of Roger's house and had kept her in the loop.

Everyone had gotten what they deserved, her included. And she was miserable.

What was that?

Sally was almost positive she heard someone say her name. She cleared her head and looked around the conference room. The other agents stared at her. This was embarrassing. Her thoughts had gotten the best of her and she had missed something important that Phillip had said. He stood there, obviously waiting for her to say something.

Did he ask me a question?

The best thing to do would be to throw out an answer. Hopefully it was a yes-or-no question, which meant she had a fifty-fifty chance of answering it correctly. She crossed her fingers and let it fly.

"Absolutely, Phillip."

The roar of laughter in the room made her jump. Guess she gave the wrong answer. The laughter faded and some of her coworkers wiped their eyes. She didn't think this situation was funny at all.

Not one bit.

Phillip moved around the table, closer to Sally. "Do you

even know what I said?"

Sally grimaced. "Not a clue."

More laughter.

"I said you looked tired. Then I asked you if you wanted a pillow."

"I see." She thought about it for a few seconds. "So, technically, my answer of *absolutely* was correct then."

A few more giggles from her coworkers.

"It wasn't the answer I wanted to hear, but yes, it was technically correct." Phillip winked at Sally and clapped his hands. "Okay, meeting's over. Everyone have a productive day. And someone get Sally a pillow."

The coworkers laughed as they filed out of the conference room. Portia and Phillip stayed behind with Sally.

Phillip pointed to Sally. "Portia, I'm worried about our friend here. She doesn't have the same spunk around the office. Not only do I miss it, I can also see it's affecting her work. She's dragging around this place like a snail."

Portia moved closer to Sally and rubbed her on the back. "I miss my spunky friend, too."

Sally stood and sighed. "You two quit being so dramatic. I'm fine. I just haven't been sleeping well, that's all."

Phillip put his hand on her shoulder. "Take a few days off if you have to. Do whatever you need to do. This isn't healthy."

After Phillip left the conference room Portia sat down in the chair next to Sally. "He's right. You need to do something."

Sally sighed. "You know better than anyone you can't just flip a switch to mend a broken heart. How many times has yours been broken? Five? Six?"

"That's irrelevant now that I'm happy again. But in *your* case, your broken heart is repairable. You just need to go over to Roger's store. Tell him you love him and you can't live without him."

"No way! He won't take me back and I'll feel like a bigger fool when he rejects me again."

"How do you know he won't take you back?"

"Because I heard it in his voice that night on the phone. He was done with me. *Disgusted* with me. And I don't blame him! Plus, if he really cared or had feelings for me, he would've at least called or stopped by."

"Why is he the one that has to make the move? You're the one who made the mistake. Plus, men are stubborn. You know that. Of course, now that I think about it I should just throw that last point out the window because you're just as stubborn as he is."

Sally didn't want to have this conversation. She already felt horrible enough without it. It's not like she hadn't thought about going to see him. She *wanted* to see him. She'd seen him more than a few times as she drove down Big Basin Way. In his favorite chair, eating his tuna sandwich at Highway 9 Sandwiches. She just wanted to pull the car over, walk up to his table, grab him, and kiss him until he forgave her. But she always imagined he'd push her away with a look of disgust on his face.

"I love him," said Sally. "Truly."

"Truly, madly, deeply . . . I know! And *he* loves *you*, too. This is so fixable, but one of you has to make the first move, and that someone is you. You think he's happy right now without you?"

Sally sighed.

"He's not," Portia continued. "I know that for a fact. Jeffrey told me he's *mis*erable. And the Mr. Crotchety that you helped make disappear is now back. Stronger and more crotchety than ever."

Sally chuckled. "It's not the real him. He's a wonderful, wonderful man."

Portia rubbed her on the back again. "Your eyes sparkle when you talk about him. You two were made for each other, believe me—don't give up. Go to him. Tell him how you feel. *The truth.* You know where he'll be at lunchtime, so just do it!"

Sally hugged Portia. "Thanks. I'll think about it."

"Oh no, you don't. Thinking is not allowed. Just do it."

Sally thought about it for a few moments. "You're right, you're right. Why not? It's better than me sitting around here like a zombie."

"Amen, sista!" She glanced down at Sally's clothes and crinkled her nose. "But you need to go home and change. You're looking a little too corporate right now. Time to turn on the sexy and give that black dress of yours an encore presentation."

"No way."

"Hey, you need to pull out the heavy artillery—no more messing around. We know what that black dress did to Roger the last time, and in his current vulnerable state it'll bring that man to his knees."

"No. I can't do that. If I want to do it right I can't have distractions or have him make a decision for the wrong reason. We need to talk heart to heart. That's the only way there will be a chance of us surviving."

Roger was tired of his nephew's psychology crap and needed to put him in his place with a few choice, highly intelligent words. "Eat my shorts."

Okay, maybe he could have done better than that but he just didn't have the energy. He hadn't slept well the last couple of weeks. It had nothing to do with being in a new house and everything to do with Miss Ham & Swiss.

He missed Sally.

The door opened and Roger turned to look. It was the teenage girl who had put the poster up in his window a month ago for the walk for cancer.

She pointed to the poster. "Hi, Mr. Hudson. We can take the poster down now." She dropped a canvas bag on the floor that appeared to hold posters she had taken down from other locations.

Roger placed the shoe horn back on the shelf. "How did you do?"

"I raised nine hundred dollars."

"I'm impressed."

"Yup. My goal was a thousand, so I almost got it. Mom says I should be proud because there are a lot of kids who would rather play video games than help with a good cause."

Roger glanced at the girl's mom outside on the sidewalk talking on her cell phone as usual. "Your mother's right. You did good."

The girl moved toward the display window to remove the poster.

Roger pointed to the glass. "Remember, smudge marks ___"

"Make you twitchy. I know." She opened the canvas bag on the floor and pulled out a pair of rubber gloves. She slipped them on her hands and smirked at Roger. She pulled the poster from the window, folded it, and stuck it in the bag. Roger could see marks on the window left from the clear tape but he decided to not say anything. It took a lot of energy to be crotchety and he was tired.

The girl turned to Roger. "Can I give Crouton a bacon treat before I go?"

"You know where they are."

The girl smiled and walked behind the counter, grabbing

the bag of treats. At the sound of the plastic bag Crouton popped up from his bed and wagged his curly little tail. "Arf! Arf!"

"Just one," said Roger. "He's so fat now I have to roll him into bed at night."

"He looks the same as he always does."

She was right, but Roger wasn't going to admit it. When he complained about others it made him temporarily feel better about his own pathetic life.

The girl gave Crouton the treat and scratched him under the chin. Then she reached up and kissed Roger on the cheek. "Thank you, Mr. Hudson."

Roger waved off her gratitude. "Don't text and drive."

"I don't have my license yet."

"Then don't drive."

She laughed. "Any other words of wisdom?"

"Yeah. Don't smoke cigarettes."

The girl rolled her eyes. "Do you really think someone who raises money to fight cancer would smoke cigarettes?"

"You'd be surprised. The doctor who treated Macy smoked two packs a day."

The girl narrowed her eyes. "I don't get that."

"That makes two of us. Hey, wait a minute." Roger opened the drawer to grab his wallet. He pulled out a hundred dollar bill and handed it to the girl.

The girl beamed. "I hit my goal!" She reached up again and kissed Roger on the cheek. "Thank you!"

"You're welcome. You're a good kid."

After the girl left Jeffrey set the feather duster on the counter. "Where were we?"

Roger huffed. "We were absolutely nowhere. Just like earlier today. Just like yesterday. And just like the day before."

"Oh, that's right. You were telling me to eat your shorts. Okay, first of all, you rarely wear shorts so I'm quite surprised you would even make that offer. And secondly——"

"Has anyone ever used a stun-gun on you? I need to get me one of those. Maybe they sell them on Amazon . . ." Roger logged into his computer.

Jeffrey got his notebook and clicked his pen. "More threats of violence. Subject has appeared to have gone off the deep end."

"Don't call me a subject. I'm your uncle. For now, at least." Roger grabbed the glass cleaner and paper towels from the cabinet in the bathroom. When he returned to the main floor Jeffrey stuck out his arm and stopped him.

"Okay, *Uncle* Roger. I wasn't going to say anything, but I think I have to at this point. Sally hasn't been well."

The bottle of glass cleaner and paper towels fell to the floor. "What? What happened? Did she have a relapse? Did the cancer return?"

Jeffrey waved his palm in the air. "No! Nothing like that."

Roger put his palm on his chest and took a deep breath, letting it out slowly. His heart pounded. It would kill him if anything ever happened to Sally.

"You scared the crap out of me!" Roger grabbed the bottle of glass cleaner and paper towels from the floor. He placed them on the counter and pointed at Jeffrey. "Don't you ever do that again."

"Hey! I said she wasn't feeling well. You were the one who jumped to conclusions and assumed the worse. The truth is she's heartbroken, which in many ways can be more painful than many common physical ailments. She's heartbroken because of you. She can't sleep and—"

"Her, too?"

"Yes! Isn't this telling you something loud and clear? You can't sleep. *She* can't sleep. You want me to get out the calculator or can you add this up on your own?"

No calculator needed. Roger had a hole in his heart. He missed Sally.

Yes, he was disappointed in her for what she had done but he also had felt guilt. Conflicted. He was pretty firm with Sally on the phone, but he should've at least given her the chance to explain. She had lied, but maybe he needed to try to understand it from her point of view. Why she had done it.

Roger paced back and forth in the store. "I should've let her explain. I was an idiot. I miss that woman so much I want to scream."

"Forget screaming. *Do* something about it. Talk with her. Ask her why she did what she did. Communicate. You may find there was a very logical reason behind it."

"A logical reason for lying?"

"Yes."

"What are you saying? Do you know something I don't know?"

"I'm going out with her best friend, so what do you think?"

"Tell me."

"No. You need to clear things up with her yourself. I'll tell you this, though. I have it on good authority she'll be eating her lunch across the street today."

Roger shot a glance through the window at Highway 9 Sandwiches. "Today?"

"Today."

Roger's body buzzed with adrenaline. He hadn't seen Sally since their celebration dinner two weeks ago. He'd continued to eat lunch across the street and deep down he'd hoped to see her, but no.

Not even once.

His heart beat even faster. What if she did show up today? What would he say? What she did was wrong, but he wanted to know why she did it. Hopefully, he wouldn't let his emotions get in the way and say something he'd regret. Maybe it would be best to let her do all of the talking.

Roger straightened his tie and smoothed out his hair. Then he checked his breath.

"Very interesting," said Jeffrey, writing in his notebook.

"Stick a sock in it." Roger frantically searched below the

214

register. "Have you seen my cologne?"

Jeffrey grinned. "In the back. On the shelf between Chanel and Jimmy Choo."

Chapter Nineteen

An hour later, Roger sat at his usual table with his usual tuna sandwich and took a bite. The sandwich tasted different today.

Much different.

He wouldn't be surprised if that pimple-faced kid inside had messed up it up again. But Roger had been so distracted with Sally on the brain he hadn't watched the employee prepare the sandwich like he normally did. Hell, he didn't even remember ordering the damn thing.

Didn't matter.

It's not like he had an appetite. He took another bite anyway and waited for Sally to arrive. He was a big bundle of nerves. He placed the palm of his hand on the top of his leg and pressed down hard after he realized it was bouncing up and down, out of control. Hopefully, she wouldn't be too much longer because he was running out of patience and there was a good chance he would—

"What a beautiful day!" yelled the familiar voice, causing Roger to clench his fist on the bag of chips, crushing them all into small pieces. He placed the smashed bag on the table and glanced up at the woman he hadn't seen in two weeks.

She placed her hand on his shoulder. "I'm glad you're here. We need to talk." She smiled and leaned toward him. "I'll be right back."

She went inside and Roger thought about her smile. It wasn't the same. It didn't have the same intensity that it normally had. It looked like she was up in her head as much as he was. He missed Sally to pieces. What a woman. Still, there was that thing of her being a liar and someone he couldn't trust. Hopefully she would explain why she did such a thing. He needed to know what had happened and he needed closure.

A few minutes later, Sally came back out with her ham and Swiss and sat at the table across from Roger. She eyed his food. "What happened to your tuna sandwich?"

"I have no idea."

Sure it tasted like hell, but at least it wasn't soggy and covered in root beer this time. He poured some potato chip crumbs from the bag into the palm of his hand and popped them in his mouth. Then he took another bite of his sandwich and chewed slowly. It usually wasn't this difficult to eat tuna.

She leaned even closer and her eyes got wider. "I know! There's paper inside of your sandwich!"

Roger's chewing slowed and then came to a halt. He pulled the top piece of bread off his sandwich and inspected it. Sure enough, there was paper inside. That clown employee had no idea how to wrap a sandwich. Roger grabbed his napkin and pretended to wipe his mouth. But what he really did was spit the bite of sandwich back out into the napkin. He folded it and tucked it in the corner of the basket.

Sally pointed to his sandwich. "You never can have too much fiber."

Sally wanted to die. She had a simple plan of apologizing to Roger and explaining her side of the story. Instead she talked about tuna sandwiches and fiber. It was pathetic.

Why was she so nervous? Why couldn't she just come out and say sorry? Say why she acted like a fool? Because she was afraid of being rejected again.

You're fired.

Never had two words stuck with her more.

She took a big breath in. It was time to quit stalling and just do it.

"I'm sorry, Roger. So very sorry for lying to you."

There. She did it.

He looked over at her and studied her for a moment and then looked across the street at his store. Maybe he was waiting for her to continue.

Keep going. Don't stop now.

"I've been in love with the Fuscos' house ever since I was a little girl. It was my dream house. My Barbie house, if you will. I have so many special memories there." She forced a smile and avoided eye contact with Roger. "We didn't live in the neighborhood, actually. My father was a gardener and the Fuscos were one of his clients. Since they were on his Saturday schedule he used to always bring me along. I was Daddy's little helper. Sometimes I raked or helped in other ways and other times I would just swing and watch him work. Tammy and William Fusco were generous and would always give me little gifts . . . dolls, candy, things for my hair. They even invited us to some of the neighborhood parties, even though we lived clear across town. I know it doesn't make a difference now, but I wanted to tell you it was more than just me loving that house as a child. My father told me I would never be able to own it because people like us couldn't afford houses like that. We never had a lot of money. I guess I kind of took it as a challenge to prove to him I could do it. I'm not sure why I continued to have an interest in that house long after he died." She tore her napkin into small pieces and fought back the tears. "Maybe I wanted to prove to myself I was worthy and capable of buying it. But I think the main reason is because I did and still do truly love that house. I feel a connection with it—as silly as it sounds. That doesn't make the lying excusable, but I just wanted you to know the whole story. I've been saving every penny for years, just waiting for the house to go on the market. I knew the Fuscos were getting up there in age and it would only be a matter of time. I wanted the house. I had to have it."

Roger nodded. "That's why you told me you didn't think the house was for me. Why you made up the excuses about the termites and them being out of town. And not being able to get ahold of their agent. You wanted the house for yourself."

That wasn't a question. It was a statement.

Roger ran his fingers through his hair. "Why didn't you just tell me? I would've stepped aside and let you have the house in a heartbeat. I could have found another place. Yes, I was interested in that particular home but not *that* much. I could've let it go." He sighed. "I have a problem with dishonesty. A huge problem. And I don't tolerate it."

Sally felt bad, but he was right. She misled him. She should've just come clean the moment he expressed an interest in the house. Now look at the mess she was in.

Tears traveled down her face. "I'm feeling pretty horrible right now. And guilty."

"Geez, Louise. Don't cry." He pulled a napkin from the dispenser and handed it to her.

"Thank you." She wiped her eyes and sniffled a couple of times. "I didn't plan on crying, but I'm a girl and these things happen without warning sometimes."

Roger grunted. "I'm going to tell you something I've never told anyone else before."

She sniffled again. "Okay."

He pushed the sandwich basket to the middle of the table and turned his chair toward Sally. "My wife Macy lied to me." He paused for a moment and cleared his throat. "She was a wonderful wife who I loved with all my heart, but she lied and it tore me apart. Sure, people may think some particular lies don't do damage. Maybe some of them don't. But many *do*. In her case, she didn't tell me she had cancer at the beginning. She kept it from me for six months. Six months! And when the cancer progressed to a certain point she had no choice but to say something, because I noticed changes in her. Her energy. Her body language. Her body. I knew something was wrong and I asked her countless times, but she just kept telling me she was overworked and needed a vacation. She said she didn't want to tell me about the cancer because it was too negative and she didn't think it was fair to put that burden on me. She wanted us to keep living our lives as if nothing was wrong. She didn't want to worry me, but she was living a lie." He sucked in a breath and let it out slowly. He shook his head and continued. "I would've lived my life differently those six months if she had told me. I would've sold the store, certainly. I would've traveled the world with her. I would've taken her every place she had ever wanted to see. And I would've done everything possible to make sure she was okay. Comfortable. Happy. Feeling more loved than ever. I'm confident I showed her how much I loved her every single day, but I would've found a way to give her more. Because of that lie I only saw the worse side of her cancer. The treatments. The mastectomy. The loss of hair. And finally the discovery of more cancer before her rapid decline. It was horrible. Absolutely horrible. So when *you* lied to me it brought those painful memories back. And then my mind told me that if you lied *once* you could surely do it again. Let's say, God forbid, you had a relapse. What if you didn't tell me? I couldn't allow myself to go through that again. It was hell. Yes, it's hell for the person going through cancer, but it's hell for everyone involved. Family, friends, everyone. And as disgusting and terrible as cancer is, it's much harder for me to deal with dishonesty. Maybe that's wrong but that's the way my mind works at this point in my life, so I'm sorry. Cancer tears apart a body. Dishonesty tears apart a relationship. It's something I won't stand for. Not now. Not ever."

Sally's eyes had already filled with tears, but now they were streaming down her face. She was the biggest fool in the world. Roger had been to hell and back and she had almost sent him on a return visit. She couldn't find the words to respond to what he had just told her. It didn't matter. He said he wouldn't stand for dishonesty and who could blame him for that? Honesty was a good value to uphold and she blew it. Not even her black dress or her legs could save her from this blunder.

I guess that's my cue.

She wrapped up the other half of her sandwich and placed it on the table in front of Roger. She glanced in his direction one more time. "You're a wonderful man, Roger Hudson." Sally felt a second round of tears on the way and needed to make a quick departure before it ruined her makeup even more. She took a step toward the sidewalk and was yanked back. She glanced down and Roger had a hold of her wrist.

He stood and faced her. "Where the hell do you think you're going?"

"I—"

"Apology accepted."

Sally jerked her head back and blinked a couple of times. More tears. The man was crazy. She had a mountain of emotions running through her body.

Apology accepted.

She took a deep breath and sniffled. That was a good thing. A *great* thing. And a step in the right direction. But what was he going to say now? Take care? That they could still be friends? *Good luck in all your future endeavors!*

Roger lowered his grip from her wrist to her hand. Then he grabbed her other hand.

Oh.

Sally's heart rate sped up. "Please say something or I'm going to pass out. Some kind of sign of what's going on in that head of yours. Apology accepted and . . ."

Roger chuckled. "That's right. Communication. It's not enough that I forgave you?"

"It was enough before. It's what I hoped for. But now that you're holding my hands and standing so close to me . . . well, that kind of gives a woman hope. So tell me something.

Anything. Just to let me know exactly what you're thinking or where we stand."

Roger pulled her closer and kissed her on the forehead. "I love you."

Sally smiled and closed her eyes. She took in the words and savored them.

I love you.

The words were magical.

More tears came. Before she could wipe her eyes or even open them Roger's lips were on hers. Just an hour earlier she had felt hopeless and tired and lonely, but now she felt alive. Roger deepened the kiss and moaned. She matched his moan and pulled him closer. She didn't want this kiss to end. They were engaged in a public display of affection and she didn't care who saw them. This was heaven.

I love you.

She wanted to hear those words again and again.

"Well, look at you two!" said Maggie. "Now that's a kiss!"

Oh, my God.

Sally had no intention of breaking the kiss off just because Maggie was there—she was enjoying it too much. Roger would have to be the one to cut it off. Surprisingly, he didn't. He deepened the kiss even more and ran his fingers through her hair, which gave her goose bumps on the back of her neck.

"Maybe it's not a kiss at all," Maggie continued. "Roger,

are you giving her mouth-to-mouth?"

Roger didn't answer. Maybe Maggie would just get the hint and go away.

"No, it can't be mouth-to-mouth," Maggie continued. "Typically the person is unconscious and on the ground. You two are having a field day here. To be honest, I don't think I've ever seen two grown adults make out here before. Especially two people as old as the two of you."

Roger grunted and Sally laughed in his mouth.

He pulled away from the kiss and turned to Maggie. "You're killing my mojo here, Maggie."

"Well, I don't even know what that is and I don't think I want to know. Just like Dr. Jenkins told me he doesn't want anybody to know he was caught nude on Prospect Road again."

"How wonderful of you to disrespect his wishes."

"This time he wasn't roller-skating, though. He was jogging! Can you imagine his package bouncing around all over the place while he runs?"

"I have better things to do with my imagination. But if you want something juicy to talk about, I've got a news flash for you. Feel free to spread it across town."

Maggie stepped forward, her eyes grew wide. "Yes?"

"Roger Hudson is in love with Sally Bright."

Maggie's eyes grew wider as they darted back and forth between Roger and Sally.

Sally held her head up high. "And Sally Bright is in love

with Roger Hudson."

Roger's head whipped over to Sally. "Pardon me?"

"What?"

"You never said anything."

"It's hard to speak when someone else's mouth is covering yours. But I just said it."

"Technically you said it in third person, so that doesn't count."

"Oooh, I like this," said Maggie. "It's like I'm watching live theater or some reality TV show. Please continue."

Sally wrapped her arms around Roger's neck and smiled. "I love you."

Roger grinned and placed a hand next to his ear. "I'm sorry, I didn't quite hear what you said."

"She said she loved you," said Maggie.

Roger narrowed his eyes at Maggie. "It's not the same coming from you. Do you mind?"

"So, you're saying you want some alone time with Sally?"

"That's exactly what I'm saying."

Maggie seemed to consider leaving. "Okay. I think I understand." She stepped off to the side and sat down in Roger's chair. She picked up Sally's leftover sandwich and smelled the paper. "You gonna finish this?

Roger grunted.

Chapter Twenty

Two weeks later, Sally awoke on a Saturday morning to get ready to spend the day with Roger.

The *entire* day.

Typically Saturdays were reserved for work, just like the other six days of the week. Especially ever since she wanted to buy the Fuscos' house. But today was a completely different day. And it was a first.

No work at all.

Roger had insisted Sally take the day off. At first she had said no. Then she had said no again. And again. And again. Some habits were just too hard to break. But it wasn't until Roger grunted and threatened to withhold his kisses did she really start to throw around the idea of actually not working.

It felt odd not getting ready for work. And exhilarating, to be honest. Roger told Sally he had something special planned and she needed to keep the entire day open. Evening, too. He also said to be ready at ten in the morning.

The last two weeks had been amazing and the two of them were inseparable.

And Mr. Crotchety was history.

In his place was the most wonderful, loving man she had ever met.

She eyed the clock on the nightstand. 9:55 a.m.

Time to get a move on.

His instructions were simple: be ready at ten and don't

worry about what to wear as long as it was casual. She threw on some jeans and a casual white blouse with sandals.

At exactly ten the doorbell rang.

She checked her hair in the mirror one last time and headed to the front door. She swung open the door and froze. It wasn't Roger.

"Sally Bright?"

It was a young man dressed in a tuxedo and hat. Funny, he looked kind of like a chauffeur. She glanced over his shoulder and there was a classic white Mercedes Benz limousine parked on the street.

"Yes, I'm Sally," she said tentatively.

"I'm Zeke Falcone. Your driver."

"Driver?"

"That's right, ma'am."

She blinked. "Sorry . . . you're not who I expected."

"I understand. I was instructed to give you *these* and ask you to open the first one."

The chauffeur handed her two envelopes. Both envelopes were numbered and next to each number was a red heart.

Now she was more confused than ever.

She glanced over Zeke's shoulder again. "I'm sorry, is Roger in the limo?"

Zeke cleared his throat and gestured toward the envelopes. "Maybe the answer's in there."

"Okay." She turned the first envelope over and tore it open with her index finger. She removed a letter from the inside. She looked back up to Zeke who smiled.

What's going on here?

She then turned her attention back to the letter and unfolded it.

Dear Sally. My love.

I've planned a very special day for you today. You've been working too hard for too long and you need to disconnect. Please remove any thoughts of work from your brain. Today, you're going to be pampered. Please get inside the limo and open envelope number two.

Love, Roger

Roger wanted to pamper Sally? She didn't have a problem with that. Just the thought made her giggle. Sally folded the letter and stuck it back in the envelope. "I guess I'm getting in your limo, Zeke."

"Very good, ma'am. Follow me."

Sally locked her front door and followed Zeke to the street. He opened the back door and she slid across the white leather seat. Her eyes traveled around the beautiful interior with its cherry wood and bamboo paneling. She smiled and pressed the overhead button and watched as the sunroof slid open.

Zeke got in the front seat and eyed Sally in the rear view mirror. "I can't leave until you open envelope number two, ma'am."

"Right!" Sally tore open the second envelope and pulled out the letter inside.

Dear Sally,

I trust that since you're reading this you made it safely from your porch to the inside of the limo on the street. Your next task is to prepare two mimosas from the drink compartment. Keep one for yourself

and place the other one in the drink holder.

Love, Roger

Sally loved this. It felt kind of like a scavenger hunt, but without all the figuring out. She prepared the two mimosas and placed one in the drink holder as Zeke drove. She looked forward to seeing Roger and toasting him. The day had just started and she was already having a wonderful time. She leaned back and relaxed in the seat with the champagne glass in her hand. This was exciting. She took a sip of her mimosa and stared out the window, wondering where they were going. It was in the opposite direction of Roger's house.

Sally leaned forward to the edge of her seat. "Zeke, where are we going?"

Zeke glanced at her in the rear view mirror and then got his eyes back on the road. "I'm not at liberty to say, ma'am. I was told when you asked me that I should tell you to relax and have another sip of your mimosa." Zeke smiled.

Roger knew her well. She did as instructed and relaxed, taking another sip.

A few minutes later Zeke pulled the limo over. Sally looked out the window and did a double take. She was so distracted she hadn't even noticed Zeke had driven to Portia's house. Portia stood on the sidewalk right outside the limo with a huge smile on her face.

Zeke jumped out and grabbed Portia's shoulder bag and stuck it in the trunk. He opened the door for her and she slid inside the limo next to Sally.

Portia screamed. "Ready for some fun?" She hugged Sally and kissed her on the cheek. Then she snapped a picture of her with her phone. Next, they took a selfie before Portia grabbed the other mimosa from the drink holder and held it in front of her. "Cheers!"

Sally clinked her glass and was more confused than ever. "I don't get it. Where's Roger?"

"I have no idea!" Portia opened her purse and pulled out a few more envelopes. She handed them to Sally. "I guess you need to open envelope number three."

Sally set her mimosa in the drink holder and opened the third envelope as Zeke drove.

Dear Sally,

You're probably wondering where the hell I am. Good, then you haven't figured out my devious plan yet. Enjoy this time with your best friend and open envelope number four when you get to your next destination.

Love, Roger

A few minutes later Zeke pulled directly in front of Sally's favorite spa. "You've got to be kidding me." She turned to Portia. "Massages?"

Portia didn't answer and pointed to the envelopes.

"Of course." Sally opened envelope number four and read it out loud.

Dear Sally,

You and Portia will now enjoy massages at your favorite place. Everything has been prepaid, including the tip, so just enjoy this time of pampering. Once you're done with the massage they will do your nails. Hint: Get a French manicure.

*You'll find out why later. You have exactly two hours
here. Go!*

Love, Roger

Sally turned to Portia. "Did you know about this?"

"The only thing I know is that man's a keeper. And I
think that's all *you* need to know."

Sally took another sip of her mimosa as Zeke opened the
door. "I already knew that! But how does he know anything
about French manicures?"

"Quit asking so many questions and let's go get our
massages!"

They slid out of the limo and Portia snapped a selfie of
the two of them in front of the door. Then they went inside
the spa.

Two hours later Sally and Portia emerged from the spa,
relaxed, rejuvenated, and starving. Fortunately, Roger had
thought of that with envelope number five.

Dear Sally,

*I hope you enjoyed the massage and you're happy
with the way your nails turned out. It's time to eat!
Zeke will now take you to your favorite restaurant.
Use the enclosed gift card to take care of the bill. At
the end of your meal, open envelope number six at
the table in the restaurant. Enjoy!*

Love, Roger

Sally looked back in the envelope and pulled out a gift
card for The Cheesecake Factory. "Okay, I never told him

this was my favorite place to eat." She flashed the card at Portia. "Confess."

"Maybe a little birdie told him."

"How much do you know?"

"Quit being so analytical. Just enjoy the day, would you?"

"I *am* enjoying the day—it's amazing. But how much longer can this go on? And when do I get to see Roger so I can give him the biggest kiss of his life?"

"You'll have plenty of time for kissing. Let's eat before I pass out."

Zeke drove the two to The Cheesecake Factory in the Valley Fair Shopping Center and dropped them off in front. She wondered what people would think when a Mercedes Benz limo pulled up to the mall, but she didn't care. She loved this restaurant.

The meal was fabulous, as usual. Sally had the Chicken Madeira while Portia opted for the Shrimp Scampi. Portia had the waiter take a picture of the two of them during the meal. Finally, it was time to wrap it up so Sally paid with Roger's gift card and stood.

Portia stopped her. "Not yet. Sit back down. You need to open envelope number six."

Sally raised an eyebrow. "Here?"

"That's what the last letter said!"

Sally sat back down and opened the next envelope, reading the letter out loud.

Dear Sally,

I hope you enjoyed your Chicken Madeira.

Sally raised her gaze to Portia and stared at her.
"What?" asked Portia.

"How did he know I ordered Chicken Madeira?" She looked around the restaurant. "Is he here?"

"Of course not. How could he be here? We've had the envelopes the entire time. Anyway, he wrote those yesterday, so it's impossible that—"

Portia cut herself off and took another sip of her iced tea.

Sally pointed to Portia. "Aha! Yesterday what? You were with him? Tell me, tell me!"

"No! Finish reading the letter. We're on a tight schedule here."

"Fine."

She glanced back down to the letter and continued to read.

Next, you and Portia are going to walk through the mall to Nordstrom. Please buy a nice dress to wear for dinner this evening with the gift card in this envelope. Don't worry about the shoes because Zeke has those in the trunk for you. Take them along so you make sure they match the dress. The only thing you have to know is the dress needs to be red. Portia will help you pick it out. Make it sexy and elegant, just like you. But not as sexy as that black dress of yours because I'm not sure my heart can handle it. On second thought, just as sexy as the black dress. Please. At least I'll die with a smile on my face. You have two hours. Happy shopping!

Love, Roger

Sally tried to analyze how much planning had to go into this day so that everything fell into place. The timing, the gift cards, the letters . . .

"You have a funny look on your face," said Portia.

"I think I'm going to cry."

"No, no, no, no! Don't do that. This is a happy day!"

"I know it's a happy day! And they'll be happy tears! I've never had a man ever do something so wonderful and sweet. It's just . . . Roger has put so much time and effort into making sure I have a day away from work to be pampered. Look at what he's done!"

"I'm looking! And lucky for me I get to enjoy it, too! Now suck it up and let's walk to Nordstrom and get you that dress."

Sally was able to control the tears. That was a close one.

Zeke opened the trunk and handed Sally the bag with the shoes.

She had to peek inside the bag, of course. "Oh, my God."

Sally's mouth hung open as she pulled the box out to show Portia.

Portia screamed. "Manolo Blahnik!"

Sally was speechless. She was well aware of how much those shoes cost. And they were gorgeous. Of course, Roger knew her size, too.

She shook her head. "This is too much."

Portia hugged Sally and laughed. "Don't be silly! You deserve every bit of this. And I'm sure you'll find more than a few ways make him feel just as special." Portia winked.

Sally laughed. "You're bad."

They walked through the mall toward Nordstrom and Sally took in a deep breath. It felt like Christmas to her. The only difference was she was on the receiving end of the presents. Like Roger kept handing her present after present after present and she wondered when it would end. Plus, how could she ever return the favor to him? No way she could ever match what he had planned. Not even close.

Almost two hours later Sally and Portia came out of Nordstrom, a bag in each of their hands. Portia had decided to splurge on a dress, too, and they'd had a wonderful time trying them on. They had taken many pictures of each other trying on the various dresses. It felt like that scene in *Pretty Woman* where Julia Roberts went dress shopping. Funny, Julia Robert's dress was also red in the movie.

They got back in the limo and Sally shuffled through the envelopes.

Only two left.

Portia pointed to the next one. "Open it."

Sally tore open the envelope and read the next letter.

Dear Sally,

Did you have fun shopping? Yeah, I know. What a question! That's like asking a monkey if he likes bananas. No, I didn't just call you a monkey! Okay, Zeke will now take you back home to get ready for our dinner. You'll have plenty of time since dinner is not until sunset. Zeke has a cooler with some wine and cheese for you in case you get hungry before then. You're getting close to your final destination!

Love, Roger

What a day it had been. And to think Sally had thought she'd be spending the entire day with Roger. Well, finally she would see him. She was so excited she was going to burst. How could this man know so much about what a woman wanted? She glanced over to her best friend, who had a smug look on her face.

"How much help did Roger need with this? I mean, come on. This has been the most amazing day ever. I've never felt so loved. Not once the entire day did I think about work. That's a miracle, I'm telling you."

Portia shrugged. "I didn't help him."

"Not one bit?"

"Okay, maybe I told him about the French manicure."

"I knew it!"

"But that was it. I just had to make sure you had nails that wouldn't clash with the dress and shoes, nothing more. He thought and planned everything else on his own. That man loves you so much it's crazy. What did you do to him?"

Sally laughed. "I have no idea, but it's the greatest feeling ever."

They arrived at Sally's place and they went in to get ready. She hadn't had this much girl time with Portia in years and it was the best. They popped open the bottle of wine and took their time getting ready as Portia told her how much she enjoyed Jeffrey's company.

"I'm in love with him," said Portia. "He's an amazing man."

"I knew you'd fall for him! What about the age difference? Any issues there?"

"None. He's very mature for his age, but still has that playful side. I'm so happy."

Sally hugged Portia. "And I'm so happy for you. You deserve it."

Portia smiled. "You do too." Portia suddenly lost her smile. "Shit!" She lunged for the box of tissues and handed one to Sally.

Soon they were both crying. Then they laughed hysterically about the crying.

Sally sniffled and reached over, wiping Portia's eyes. "You're a mess."

Portia reached over and wiped Sally's eyes. "You're one to talk."

They laughed and continued to get ready. Thank God, no more tears.

Just before sunset they walked back outside where Zeke patiently waited. He opened the door for them and drove to the final destination.

The more Zeke drove the more Sally had a sneaking suspicion as to where they were going. He traveled down Cox Avenue over the railroad tracks and made a left on Seagull Way. Then a right on Yuba Court.

"I knew it," said Sally.

Zeke parked the Mercedes Benz in front of the former Fusco property, now the Hudson house. She had spent a lot of time there the last couple of weeks and was more in love with the house than ever.

Zeke ran around to the other side of the limo and opened the door for Sally and Portia. They both slid out and Sally and turned to Zeke. "Thank you. You've had a long day."

"Not at all, ma'am. The time flew by. It was fun to be a part of your adventure." He took a picture of the two of them in front of the limo and then Portia took a selfie of the three of them. Then they said goodbye to Zeke.

Portia pointed to the swing under the magnolia tree. "Last envelope. Let's go."

Sally picked up the envelope from the swing. It sat on top of a red necktie. She picked up the tie and analyzed it. "What's this for?"

"Open the envelope."

Sally opened it and pulled out the letter.

Dear Sally,

You did it! You've made it to your final destination. I hope you were able to completely disconnect from work and enjoy your day off. I guess I can tell you now that I'll be seeing you in just a few short minutes. And I can't wait to see you, my love. To hold you. To kiss you. Portia is going to blindfold you with the red tie and lead you to the backyard through the gate on the side yard. I'm waiting for you. Don't peek!

Love, Roger

Sally smiled and turned her back to Portia. "Okay. Go for it."

Portia took the red tie from Sally and wrapped it gently around her eyes. She grabbed Sally by the hand and led her thru the side gate. That's when she heard the song.

"Lady in Red" by Chris De Burgh.

"I love this song," whispered Sally.

Portia squeezed her hand. "Me, too."

The music got louder as they walked further into the backyard. They took a few more steps and Portia let go of Sally's hand.

"You just going to leave me here?"

Portia didn't answer.

Sally stood there for a few moments waiting, enjoying the romantic song.

She felt hands grab toward the back of her head, undoing the tie.

"Keep your eyes closed."

Roger.

Her heart rate sped up and she took in a deep breath, letting it out slowly. She was nervous. And excited. And she wanted to kiss the heck out of Roger.

"Okay," she whispered. "Eyes remain closed."

Her eyes were now uncovered, but she kept her word and didn't open them.

Roger grabbed her hands and pulled her close for a dance. With her eyes closed the song sounded more beautiful than ever. But after a few more revolutions she grew impatient. She wanted to see Roger's face.

"Can I open my eyes now?"

"Okay."

She opened her eyes and smiled. She stared at the most gorgeous man in the world. He was dressed in an elegant charcoal suit and wore the red necktie she had had around her eyes. She was about to reach up and kiss him when something caught her attention in her peripheral version.

Sally's mouth fell open. She stopped dancing. "I must be dreaming."

Chapter Twenty-One

Roger smiled and let go of Sally's hands. The look on her face was priceless. Her mouth still hung open and her eyes couldn't have been open any wider. She did a three-sixty and glanced around the yard at the Japanese paper lanterns he'd hung from every single tree. Over fifty of them in different colors and sizes.

"Lady in Red" ended and the only sound in the yard was from the crickets.

Sally looked stunning in her red dress. He couldn't believe this beautiful woman loved him so much. And he loved her with all his heart. Just the thought put a smile on his face and he couldn't wait any longer.

Roger dropped down on one knee.

He'd done this before, but somehow he was more nervous this time.

Sally's eyes followed him toward the ground and her hand flew up to cover her mouth. "Oh, Roger."

He cleared his throat. "Sally, my love. Having you in my life is *such* a gift. A treasure. Before I met you I was just an old goat with a bad attitude."

Sally chuckled and sniffed. Then she wiped her eyes.

"I'm a changed man," he continued. "A better man . . . because of you. Now I can see again what life is about. It's about love. It's as simple as that. Well, love is not so simple sometimes, but you get my point."

"I do."

"No, you can't say *I do* yet. Not until I pop the question."

"I was saying *I do* get your point. About love not being simple sometimes."

"Oh . . . right."

Roger heard snickering in the yard but pushed it from his mind and continued. "I'll be forever grateful for meeting you." He pulled a small box from inside his jacket pocket and flipped it open. He pulled the ring out and set the box on the ground. He ignored the flashes from the cameras in the yard. "I want to spend the rest of my life with you. Sally . . ."

"I do."

Roger grunted.

Sally crinkled her nose. "Sorry. Please continue. It's just . . . I can't wait to be engaged to you and I can't wait to be your wife. I'll be quiet now, but please do hurry."

"Sally . . ."

She opened her mouth and he held up his index finger to stop her.

"Will you marry me?"

"Yes!" Sally pulled him up and lunged forward to kiss him.

He pulled away and laughed. "You're crazy. Look, I

appreciate your enthusiasm, but I need to put this engagement ring on your finger if we're going to make it official." He slid it on and grinned. "I love you."

"I love you, too."

This time it was Roger's turn to dish out a kiss. The camera flashes went off, followed by cheers of approval from Jeffrey and Portia.

The two moved in closer and joined together, giving Sally and Roger a group hug.

"Arf! Arf! Arf!"

Roger turned toward the house. "Jeffrey, can you let Crouton out?"

"Of course."

Jeffrey slid open the glass door and Crouton sprinted in Sally's direction. She laughed and bent down to pet him. The dog said thank you with a few hundred licks. "Hey, you! Are those congratulatory kisses?"

"I'm jealous," said Roger. He pulled Sally back up and kissed her again. "Well? How did I do? Better than a banner on a trash dumpster?"

Sally laughed. "A million times better. This has been the most amazing day of my life. What you did today, all of the effort and thought and love you put into it, I'm speechless. Really. Thank you."

"My pleasure. And we don't have to wait until after the wedding for you to live here with me. Move in with me. How's tonight?"

Sally laughed. "Sounds wonderful."

"Let's talk dates!" said Portia. "The sooner the better, since I'm going to be the oldest maid of honor ever! I'm going to be your maid of honor, right?"

Sally hugged Portia. "Of course. And I'm older than you, so what are you talking about? I certainly don't feel like I'm going to be an old bride. Happiness and love have no age limit."

Roger slapped Jeffrey on the shoulder. "I want you to be my best man."

Jeffrey hugged his uncle. "I'd be honored."

"Now that that's settled, I say there certainly is no reason to have a long engagement. What do you think, my love?"

Sally kissed Roger. "I agree. How about we get married in six weeks? That's enough time for us to plan something nice and intimate."

"Six weeks it is! Okay, dinner's been keeping warm in the oven, so let's eat and let's celebrate. I'm the happiest man in the world! What a beautiful night!"

Roger heard a scribbling noise and turned to find Jeffrey writing like a maniac in his notebook. "Seriously? You couldn't leave it alone for just one day?"

"No way. This is the final chapter of my thesis and it's the best part. I'm going to graduate summa cum laude with this bad boy." Jeffrey continued to write and then chuckled.

Roger pointed to his face. "What's that smirk for? What did you just write?"

"Nothing."

"Tell me."

Jeffrey shrugged. "Fine." He turned the notebook around so Roger could read it.

As I predicted, Uncle Roger and Sally will be married within three months of meeting. Uncle Roger owes me $200.00. Sucker.

Roger grunted.

THE END

<<<>>>

A Note From Rich

Dear Reader,

I hope you enjoyed my fourth romantic comedy, *Mr. Crotchety*. What a blast it was to write. I have the best job in the world! I would be so grateful if you would leave a review online on Amazon and Goodreads. It would mean the world to me and would also help new readers find my stories.

And feel free to send me an email to say hello! I love to hear from my readers—it motivates me and helps me write faster. :) My email address is rich@richamooi.com.

With gratitude,

Rich

Acknowledgements

It would have been impossible to write and publish *Mr. Crotchety* on my own. I'd like to thank everyone who helped make it happen.

First, a big smoochy thank you to my hot Spanish wife, Silvi. She's the one I bounce ideas off of in the very beginning. If I get stuck or need a different angle on something, she's there to help. And of course she always gives me great feedback after she reads the first draft. Thank you, my honeybunch. I love you. :)

Special thanks to Michael Hauge and Hannah Jayne for the brainstorming sessions.

To my wonderful editor Mary Yakovets. Thank you for polishing everything up and making it pretty.

Thank you to Paula Bothwell for proofreading. You're the best!

To Sue Traynor for drawing another amazing cover. Thank

you so much.

To my amazing beta readers. Robert, Isabel, Krasimir, Julita, Silvi, and Deb. I give you my deepest thanks. Thank you for your friendship, support, and kindness.

To all of the amazingly-talented authors in the super-secret Facebook AC group. YOU ROCK!

To our dog Chiqui who keeps me company during that day while the wife is at work and I'm home alone writing.

Made in the USA
Middletown, DE
12 December 2018